Praise for t
Taxi For the Dead

"If you like your mystery with a paranormal edge, then you should be reading this series." ~Cheryl Green

Praise for Renaissance Faire Mysteries

"**Fatal Fairies** was a good read. I loved being back at the Renaissance Faire Village with Jessie, Chase and all of the village characters. I like the magical twist that happens to Jessie in this book and I'm curious to see what other magic happens in future books. Thank you Joyce and Jim for writing a great story that transported me to a village I wouldn't mind living in! Eagerly awaiting the next book in the series!" ~ **R. Davila**

Praise for Missing Pieces Mysteries

"I really enjoyed **A Watery Death**, it was full of a few surprises and a very nice guest appearance that was fun to read about. As well as a nice surprise but sad guest appearance to enjoy. Can't wait for the next book!" ~ **April Schilling**

Praise for the Retired Witches Mysteries

"**Spell Booked** kept me guessing. Who was good, who could be trusted, and who was the rogue witch? Joyce and James Lavene created a world where magic and mundane live together yet separate-even in the same households." ~ **Cozy Up With Kathy**

Some of our other series:

Renaissance Faire Mysteries
Wicked Weaves
Ghastly Glass
Deadly Daggers
Harrowing Hats
Treacherous Toy
Perilous Pranks—Novella
Murderous Matrimony
Bewitching Boots

Missing Pieces Mysteries
A Timely Vision
A Touch of Gold
A Spirited Gift
A Haunting Dream
A Finder's Fee
Dae's Christmas Past
A Watery Death

Taxi for the Dead Mysteries
Undead by Morning
Broken Hearted Ghoul
Dead Girl Blues

Retired Witches Mysteries
Spell Booked
Looking for Mr. Good Witch

Be My Banshee

A Purple Door Detective Agency Mystery

By

Joyce and Jim Lavene

Chapter One

The Purple Door Detective Agency is hiring.
Those without magic need not apply.
Salary commensurate with experience.
Apply at the agency on Brooke Street. No phone calls or
psychic links.

"You're next." The young assistant stood beside the ragged hag. "I mean, she can see you now." She shivered, and her nose twitched as she looked into the gaunt face.

The hag, even thinner than the young woman watching her, rose slowly to her full height—well over six feet. Her bones and joints cracked and complained at being used.

Her torn robe was shades of gray and black, covered with dust and mold. Her hair was long and gray with patches missing at her scalp. Her eyes, when she fixed them on the young woman, were only dark sockets. Her mouth had been open, revealing rotted teeth for the entire time she'd been waiting, close to two hours.

"Thank ye." She closed her mouth enough to mumble. There was a trace of Irish brogue about her sandpaper voice.

"Y-you're welcome." The young woman scurried back to her desk and licked her hand before she ran it across her face. She stopped when she realized others in the waiting room were watching her. At that point, she gulped hard and went to hide in the supply closet.

There were some of every kind there—werewolves, vampires, witches—and others she couldn't identify. They sat in the pretty purple chairs while they waited for their interviews as music played softly in the background. The word had only gone out that morning that the Purple Door Detective Agency was hiring. The turnout was everything the owner of the firm could have hoped for.

"Come in. Sit down." Sunshine Merryweather gestured to a deep purple chair opposite her desk. She was busy sorting through shoes with a frown on her beautiful face. "Tell me what you can do for me," she said for the tenth time that morning.

Sunshine was plump with a ripeness of life that showed in her bright blue eyes and pink cheeks. She had a mass of strawberry blond hair that never stayed where she put it when she tried to clasp or pull it back. It truly had a life of its own.

She was a young witch, barely seventy-five, with most of her life in front of her. She was ambitious and impatient at times. Her clothing trended toward brightly-colored retro wear that she bought in large quantities at thrift stores and sometimes wore with long, colorful capes. When it came to jewelry, more was her mantra. She loved real gemstones but wasn't above wearing good fakes. She loved to sparkle when she walked into a room.

The figure at the door hadn't moved toward the chair. Sunshine finally found the matching purple pump she'd been searching for and put it on her foot as she dropped gracefully into her purple chair.

"Do you speak?" she asked. "Not that it matters if your other abilities work for me. What can you do?"

"It is what you can do for me that has brought me here this day, witch." The hag's voice was hoarse as though she hadn't used it in a long time. When she coughed, dust came from her open mouth.

"I see." Sunshine tapped her sparkling, purple pen against her desk. "Maybe you should wait outside until the interview process is over. We're only at partial strength with the death of our associate. That's why we're having this cattle call this morning, Miss—?"

"Aine. My name is Aine. I am come from Ireland this very day. I am in need of your assistance, or you should find me a formidable enemy. Do not think to press me or waste my time."

Sunshine smiled, staring at the hag with eyes that saw everything but gave away nothing. She was powerful and could be ruthless if the need arose. She rarely bent herself to that sort of passion, but intuition told her the ancient woman in front of her might be enough to drive her to the edge.

Her lover, and the man who'd helped her start the Purple Door Detective Agency, had been brutally slaughtered three days before during a full moon. The moon phase was important to the matter because John Lancaster was a werewolf who was at the height of his power on that night. Nothing should have been able to rip him to pieces, which was how they'd found him. She wanted nothing less than extreme vengeance. But first she had to find the culprit, and that had proved annoyingly difficult.

"Look. I appreciate that you've come a long way—is that Aine? Does that rhyme with pain?" she finally said to the hag.

"No, witch. You might say it as Ann."

"But I'm really busy today," Sunshine continued. "Come back tomorrow when I have a new associate, and we'll talk about your case. Right now, you're in the way. There's a very nice bed and breakfast up the street from here. You could stay there. Leave your name when you make an appointment with my assistant at the desk outside. Thanks for being so understanding."

The hag didn't budge. She stood her ground, gazing at the witch with eyes that had not seen a sunrise in more than two hundred years. Her mouth slowly opened, and the most horrendous screech imaginable issued from it. Her garments seemed possessed of a life all their own as they stood out around her. Her shriek continued, rattling the windows in the old brick building. Gnarled, clawed hands reached toward the witch as the plaster on the walls cracked and nails dropped from the wood around them.

Sunshine didn't move or show surprise though her hair appeared as windblown as if she'd been driving her purple convertible with the top down.

"Well. That happened." She moved her chair close to the desk again. The hag's shriek had actually caused furniture to shift. "You could have told me you were a banshee. That was really impressive. Maybe we have something to talk about after all."

"'Ware me, witch." The hag appeared weakened now that it was over. "I am Aine, a past Queen of Ulster. I am doomed to follow the O'Neill family as their *beane sidhe* for my remaining time on this earth. I am stronger than you can imagine. I require your assistance and shall not be denied."

"I can see that. And I'm so sorry for saying your name incorrectly. I know how that can be. How do you say Sunshine Merryweather the wrong way? And yet people manage it."

She giggled, and Aine grimaced. Was she reduced to asking for help from this flirtatious trollop who had less sense than she ought?

Yet here she was, in a strange land far from home, possibly the last of her kind. She'd fallen into a deep slumber, no doubt magic of some sort, and had awakened alone in a rotting, abandoned castle. None of the branch of the O'Neill family she served was to be found in the land of her birth. Her unerring sense of knowing where to find someone of the bloodline had led her thousands of miles, across the great ocean, to this city—Norfolk. It was in the land of Virginia.

While she knew the remaining O'Neill was here on these black rock roads, she wasn't able to locate him. It was possible that her long sleep had dulled her magic. But it was essential that she find him. There were secrets to whisper in his ear as she guided him to the underworld. She had also to keen before his death. If she did not do these things, her debt would not be paid and she would turn to dust when O'Neill was dead.

Unless he had a child to pass on her legacy. Now that would be heaven, or as near to it as she would ever be.

There was the faintest of taps at the door.

"Come in," Sunshine called.

No one entered.

She sighed and got to her feet, walking around Aine, to open the door. She looked down. A small, white mouse was chattering at her. Its tiny paws were held tightly against its white chest.

"Yes, I know, Jane. I'll speak to him. For goodness sake, pull yourself together. We have a whole room full of potential employees—not to mention possible customers."

The mouse nodded nervously and slowly became the young woman who'd ushered Aine into the office.

"That's much better. Thank you very much." Sunshine glanced at Aine. "Would you like some tea or coffee? I can tell you're parched, excuse the humor. Jane will get you anything you want. Jane Smith, Aine of Ulster. She's a banshee—but be careful—she's sensitive about it."

Jane gulped as she was left with Aine in Sunshine's large office. "W-would you like some tea?"

"I'm not here for tea, little mouse. Scurry away now."

Sunshine allowed the women to fend for themselves as she crossed the office to speak with another associate, Mr. Bad. She ignored the hopeful looks of potential employees, opened the door, and stepped into his office.

"I'm sorry. I need to speak to you. Who would've guessed a banshee would turn up? Not that she wouldn't make a great addition to the team. I didn't know banshees were still around. I mean, I've heard of them, but I've never met one or known anyone who has, have you?"

The room was completely dark. But she knew her partner was seated behind his huge, old desk. There was one large window in the office. It was heavily draped with thick black cotton. Not so much as a sliver of sunlight made it through that opening. There were no sounds either. Noise and light bothered Mr. Bad.

"Stop blathering." Mr. Bad's voice wheezed. "Why is she here?"

"Something about looking for someone named O'Neill. Probably from the family she haunts. She can't find him and wants our help."

"She does not seek employment?"

"No. And it's probably just as well. I know banshees are strong, but I could see from her tantrum that they can also be destructive."

"Talk her around, Miss Merryweather. We could use a force like her."

Sunshine abruptly stopped pacing the floor.

Mr. Bad never came out of his office or interfered in the daily business operations. Many times she'd asked him for his opinion and had received the barest grunt in reply.

She wasn't even sure what he looked like in the light. One morning she'd come down to work and there he'd been in the side office. No explanation or asking if she had a vacancy.

He'd talked to John. Sunshine's partner had come out of the office with a look that wavered between fear and awe.

"He has to stay, Sunny," John had said. "I-I can't explain except that he has to stay."

And so Mr. Bad—their name for him, not his—had stayed in that office. He paid rent on it the first of every month with cash on Jane's desk. Occasionally he shared some words of wisdom with John or the all-knowing grunt with Sunshine.

Until now. This time he actually had something to say even though she wasn't sure that she agreed with it.

Sunshine's temper got the better of her. "Why her? Because her voice can shake a house to the ground? Is it her charm and beauty? You never have anything to say about anything. Why now?"

"I can feel her presence from here," he wheezed. "She is of the *fae*, one of the oldest of races. The children of the goddess. It is not only her voice that has strength, my dear Miss Merryweather. Find a way to hire her. Make sure the contract is properly binding."

"Binding? The only people who work for me want to be here. You said yourself that she's a force to be reckoned with. Why would I pit my witchcraft against her magic?"

His breath rasped in his throat. "Do it. Or you will regret it. As you say, I don't interfere, but I make an exception in this case. Find a way to keep the *beane sidhe* with us."

Sunshine started to argue. She didn't like being told what to do. But she had always known Mr. Bad had an understanding of the world that she lacked. Whether it was magic, or some older force of nature, she had never witnessed his anger and never wished to.

"All right. I'll take care of it. But I hope you're ready to step in if she gets out of hand."

"Treat her with the respect she is due and nothing will happen."

The conversation was over. His slow creaking movement, turning away from her in his chair, was enough to tell her so. Sunshine left his office, walking through the waiting room of potential employees.

Who Mr. Bad was, and what his powers were, had never come up in conversation. He'd been good counsel to John in bad times and had helped 'arrange' certain matters that were outside their capabilities. He'd never confided in her or told her how he'd come to be there. John had refused to ask.

Now he believed the banshee should take John's place at the agency. She swallowed hard, at least temporarily agreeing with his ideas on the situation.

"I'm sorry," Sunshine told the crowd. "The position has been filled. If any of you are interested in hiring the agency to work for you, please stay behind, and I'll see you as soon as I can."

"Wait!" A man called out, struggling from his chair. "I can do amazing things! You should hire me."

As she watched, the man stretched his arms toward the ceiling, grasping the chandelier, and swinging from one side of the room to the other. He lost his grip and dropped abruptly to the carpet, groaning and turning his head from side to side.

"Thank you so much. Leave your card. We'll let you know the next time we're hiring."

Chapter Two

Sunshine was glad to see that Aine had finally sat in the purple chair. Jane had even convinced her to drink some tea. Did banshees eat? She was going to have to learn what she could about her new employee.

"That was Mr. Bad, another partner in the agency." Sunshine explained about him as she gathered her energy. When she opened the drawer in her desk, there was a contract there. "He's concerned about us looking for Mr. O'Neill. He'd like you to sign this contract basically saying that we aren't responsible for any physical damage that's done by you while you're working for us."

Aine put down the tea cup. She hadn't tasted the flowery-smelling brew. She couldn't remember the last time water had crossed her lips.

"I'll not sign a thing. You do what you have to and find the remaining O'Neill."

"I don't think you understand how things work today."

Sunshine took a seat behind her desk but kept a vigilant eye on the other woman. "No one does anything without a contract. We barely eat or sleep without one. It's the way of the world. Mr. Bad says we need you to sign this. I can't do any magic until you do."

Jane had been quietly waiting behind Aine. When she heard the blatant lie, she hurried from the room in case the banshee decided to screech. She'd never heard anything like it before—and never wanted to again. It had awakened all the primal fears she tried to hide every day as a human. As a mouse, her life had been filled with terrors. Just the closing of a door was enough to drive her into hiding.

Aine eyed the paper in front of her. She couldn't read anything of the odd language on it. She didn't understand what trickery the witch was attempting, but there was little the twit could do to her. She finally picked up the writing device that was put before her and signed her name.

As soon as it was on the contract, the paper immediately went up in flames and vanished in the air.

"What wizardry is this?" Aine asked her. "Don't hope to best me in a battle of wits or power. That contract is as binding for you as it is for me."

"I wish you'd learned to trust me." Sunshine held her pretty eyes wide as her curls stirred around her face. "I swear I mean you no harm. I will help you find the man you're looking for. There's just a small matter of you helping me find my associate's killer."

"What?" Aine rose halfway from the chair, her bony hands on the desk, legs creaking under her weight. "I have agreed to nothing that will help you, witch. Do your craft. Find O'Neill."

"You know, if we're going to be friends, you should start by calling me Sunshine. Or Sunny. Some of my closest friends call me Sunny. But something about the way you say 'witch' sounds derogatory to me. You may not realize it, but witches have been persecuted in the past. We like to stay away from that kind of thing now."

"Ye mean burned alive, don't ye?" Aine chuckled, not a pleasant sound. "Yes. I know. I can understand why you're so sensitive."

Sunshine winced at her words. "I'm sure you wouldn't like me to bring up past hurts that banshees have suffered— or dead Queens of Ulster."

"What is it you want of me? I have made it plain what I require of you. Don't play games with me, witch. You would find me a bad loser."

"I think we're talking at cross purposes here, Aine." Sunshine smiled at her. "You have abilities that Mr. Bad seems to feel could be useful to our investigation into our associate's death. We could help you negotiate the modern world to find your O'Neill so you can scream at him whenever you like. You help us. We help you. Is that clear?"

Aine stood up to her full height again, towering over the seemingly calm witch who didn't so much as blink one of her perfectly made-up eyes. Her jaw dropped to unleash her keening wail. But nothing came out of her throat.

"What have you done?" Aine demanded.

"You signed over temporary rights for your 'gift' to the Purple Door Detective Agency until such time as we are both satisfied that our contract is complete."

"Signed over?" Aine's skeletal hand reached for Sunshine's throat. "I shall throttle the life from your worthless body! Then I shall feed your contract to the mouse. You may control my keening, but you do not control me."

Sunshine found that Aine's words were true. She'd planned to get away so quickly that the she couldn't catch her, but once the banshee's hand had lodged around her neck, she couldn't move. She tried several types of spells, but none worked on her opponent.

"We can still be friends," she grated past the banshee's grip. "We can go shopping and find you something to wear that didn't come out of a grave."

Aine pressed her advantage over the astonished witch and would have snapped her neck. But the room around them began to shake as a voice bellowed from Mr. Bad's office.

"Enough!"

This was deep, older magic. She recognized the ancient feel of it. It had been many years since she'd known anything of its kind. The man in the other room that the witch called Mr. Bad was much more than her partner. Even though her entire being was caught up in needing to find O'Neill, she wondered who and what he really was. She might have to discover the answer for herself before she returned home.

Sunshine sat back in her chair, coughing delicately, her face pale and stunned as though unaccustomed to brute force. Aine stood back, waiting to see what the real power behind this place required of her.

"He wants us in there," Sunshine croaked.

"Does he now?" Aine sneered, her distaste at being summoned obvious.

"Come this way."

Sunshine walked across the outer office. Aine saw the small shapeshifter on the desk. To change shape and become a mouse seemed a waste of power to her. She had to wonder at the young woman's family that had allowed such a thing.

Mr. Bad was still seated in his large chair behind the desk. Aine had barely a glimpse of him as the door opened and closed behind them and they were part of his dark world.

"I know this is not what you came for, Aine," he said in a rumbling voice. "But you have my word that we will help you find the young man you seek."

"You will not manipulate me in this manner," Aine told him. "I am descended from the great kings. I came to you for help. All I have found is trickery by this puppet witch who serves you."

"Don't mistake me, Aine of Ulster. I know who you are and what crimes you have committed, which you have tried to erase through your service to the O'Neill family. I have need of you. Help us and find what you came for. Without us you will wither and die never fulfilling your obligations."

Aine didn't reply. She trembled in her fury at choosing this place to ask for assistance.

Yet something had brought her here when she couldn't locate the last O'Neill of the bloodline. No doubt it was this dark man and his witch. The smell and feel of power was all around her. She'd been drawn here and now couldn't leave until their bargain was met.

"It seems I have no choice, Dark Lord." Aine inclined her head to show her respect for the powerful elder. "But mark me well—keep your witch leashed. I have no wish to hurt her, but I shall if she annoys me past what I can endure."

"It seems we have an accord then, my lady."

Aine and Sunshine left the dark office, closing the door behind them. They stared angrily at each other, appearing to size one another up as though expecting a battle. Their gazes narrowed and their hands became fists.

Jane laughed nervously, transformed into a woman again. "Awesome. Who could eat some pizza? I don't know about you two, but I'm starved. We can go over the details of what needs to be done while we eat. What do you think?"

Her words broke their concentration. Sunshine glanced away from the banshee's face.

"Of course. Why not?" She smiled at Jane and ignored Aine.

Aine went grudgingly with the witch and the mouse, not certain what to make of this new threat. Mr. Bad stayed in his office.

The pizzeria was a few doors down in another historic, renovated brick building close to the downtown office for the Norfolk Police Department. The smell of tomatoes and spices drew the lunchtime crowd like a come-hither spell.

"Maybe we should do something with those clothes first." Sunshine stared at Aine. "We could hit the consignment shop before we eat. It's only a block or two away."

Jane carefully agreed, keeping her distance from the banshee. "This is buy one, get one free day too. She could probably use more than one outfit."

"Bah!" Aine stepped away from Sunshine and Jane, off the busy sidewalk. "The two of you prattle like magpies. If there is a need, I can appear different at any time."

Sunshine tilted her head. "Really? Please do. We know people here. I'm not sure how I'd explain bringing in a zombie to lunch."

"Stand away. Allow me to allay your misgivings about my appearance."

Aine shook herself from head to toe. Dust and dirt from the old castle fanned out around her and fell to the street.

"Why would she choose to look like that if she doesn't have to?" Jane whispered in a trembling voice.

"There's no accounting for taste," Sunshine muttered as she watched the transformation. "Besides, she was hoping to scare us. I guess she found we weren't scared so easy."

"I think she was as terrified of Mr. Big as we are."

"Hush now." Sunshine cut her off. "Let's see what she has."

Aine's appearance had changed to a more human form. Her face became fuller with pale flesh and green eyes. Her form slightly filled out the ankle-length black dress she wore, a black hood across her gray hair. Her feet were encased in rough leather sandals.

"Does this suit you?" she asked the other women.

"Not bad," Sunshine said. "It needs a scarf or some jewelry, but it'll do. Much better than the corpse. This way you almost look like a witch."

"Not exactly what I had in mind," Aine said. "There has never been a witch on the throne of Ulster."

"How do you know?" Sunshine wondered as they started walking toward the pizzeria again. "As I said, witches were persecuted in the past. They'd be unlikely to announce what they were as they ascended the throne."

They went into the trendy restaurant and were seated by an older teenager popping her bubble gum as she guided them to a table. There was a crowd for lunch, as always. It was a mixture of business types in suits and casual wear with trendy shoppers and friends meeting for a meal. There was also a fair amount of police officers.

"Isn't this awesome?" Sunshine asked Aine. She'd sat beside her in the booth while Jane shivered across from them. "I bet they didn't have anything like this where you came from."

Aine glanced around with disdain, her head held regally high as she took in the modern atmosphere. "Aye, they had nothing like this. There was a tavern where the hunt stopped that was frequented by the royals and their friends. The food was roasted boar, apples, cheese, and ale so good it made men weep."

Sunshine picked up a menu and handed it to Aine. "No boar here, but the pizza with roasted peppers is to die for. You should try it, unless you don't like spicy foods."

"I don't like spicy foods," Jane whispered from behind her tall menu. "They give me a tummy ache."

"Why does your shapeshifter turn into a mouse?" Aine asked. "Surely a valuable shapeshifter would turn into a wolf or a horse—something of power and strength."

Sunshine tapped her purple and silver nails on the tabletop. "Where's that waiter? I'm starving."

"I don't shapeshift into a mouse," Jane explained. "I'm a mouse who shapeshifts into a woman."

Aine glanced at Sunshine. "Is this true? Was it ye who cursed her this way?"

"It was an accident," she mumbled, reading the fine print on the menu. "I'm not the kind of witch who normally does magic of that sort."

"What kind are you?" Aine asked.

"The kind who tries to do good for people. That's why I

started the Purple Door Detective Agency. We solve problems for those of us outside society. It's mostly for people like us who have been wronged by humans or others of our kind. We settle disputes, locate lost relatives, that kind of thing."

As Sunshine continued outlining dozens of cases that had come to them in the past five years that the agency had been open, Aine felt a burning sensation in her head. Something was amiss. She hadn't felt that ache for so long. She almost mistook it for illness.

But it was the mark of the family she served. An O'Neill of the bloodline was close. She tried to sharpen the feeling, knowing it would lead her to him. She already knew there was only one heir—a male. He had not taken a family nor had children as yet. He was quite young himself, and alone. His affections were still free from any female who might truly engage them.

Once she'd tuned out the constant chattering of her companions, it became clear that he was there in the eating hostelry. He was among the close crowd seated and enjoying the strange food she smelled.

"Hi there!" The waitress greeted them. "Did you notice the specials at the door when you came in? No? Well, let me spell them out for you. We have a slice of deep dish cheese and pepperoni. That's served with a small salad. We have breadstick pizza. And we have pizza soup which may not sound appetizing, but trust me, it's really yummy."

Aine stood rapidly. "Stop speaking. You are disturbing my concentration. Why must you all blather constantly? Is this what the future holds?"

The waitress with the slice of pizza fascinator on her pink hair stared without speaking, a look of horror on her face, despite the more human aspect of Aine's appearance.

"We'll all have the breadstick pizza." Sunshine rapidly made the executive decision. "Three sweet teas with that, plenty of ice."

The waitress finally blinked and put the order into the tablet she held. "Thanks. We'll have that ready in a jiffy." She wasted no time moving away from their table.

"Sit down, Aine," Sunshine hissed, hoping no one was watching. "Your blood sugar is probably low after your trip from Ireland. Do banshees fly? I can't remember from the mythology. You know, you might be the only banshee left."

Aine didn't sit down. She left the table as though drawn beyond her will to discover the O'Neill she had sensed.

"What's she doing?" Jane whispered to her boss. "Is she going to scream again?"

"No." Sunshine got up. "Not on my watch. Wait here."

Chapter Three

Aine was walking slowly past the restaurant's patrons, staring into each face. She had already gone by several tables where the people stared back with looks of surprise.

"You can't do this here," Sunshine told her. "This isn't your boar-eating century. And some of these people could be clients in the future. You know what those are, right?"

"Silence, witch." Aine sniffed a man in a gray business suit. "The last O'Neill is here now. I knew he was close. I have no need of further assistance from you. I must only identify him and make it known who I am."

The assistant manager approached them. He was a young man with curly, red hair who played with his pizza tie as he spoke. "I'm sorry ladies, but could you please take your seats? You're making the other customers uncomfortable."

"We were looking for the restroom." Sunshine smiled at him. "Maybe you could find it for us." She muttered a spell to forget under her breath.

"Of course. Thank you." He smiled and walked away.

Aine put her hand on a man's balding head and turned him to face her. "You are not the man I seek."

He breathed easier that it was true and moved closer to his companion.

"You're making a spectacle of yourself," Sunshine told her. "I can find this O'Neill person much easier than this. Just give me some idea what he looks like. I'll have him come to us."

Already angry that she was having such a difficult time identifying the man she must serve, Aine turned on the witch. "Leave me be. Do you not think if I knew him I would go to him? I can yet find him without your help. I have agreed to work with you, but you sorely try my patience."

"I'll leave you alone as soon as you sit down and eat your pizza."

Aine raised her hands and opened her mouth.

"No. We aren't doing that except as the agency needs you, remember?"

But at that moment, Aine's unfailing sense located the O'Neill heir. He was seated across from a beautiful woman with black hair, creamy white skin, and eyes the color of the summer sky. He was sharing pizza soup with her.

She pushed Sunshine aside and ran to him, dropping on one knee beside his table, her head inclined with respect. "O'Neill. I find you at long last. We are united now. You need not fear your death."

Sean Patrick O'Neill barely glanced away from his girlfriend's face. "Thanks. Could you bring the extra salad back with you?"

"She's in training," Sunshine told him. "Excuse us."

"You do not recognize me," Aine continued, refusing to give up her quest. "I was under an enchantment for these past two hundred years and more. Your family—your home—has fallen into ruin. But as the last of the O'Neill bloodline, I am your *beane sidhe*. I shall haunt you to your grave and then guide you to the underworld. Have no fear. I am at your side."

Sean O'Neill, the last of a noble line that he was completely unaware of, was a handsome young man in his early thirties. His slightly curly brown hair had gold highlights, and his blue eyes viewed the situation with equanimity. His gray suit wasn't expensive, but he wore it well on a tall, lean body with broad shoulders. His mouth had smile lines, indicating his good humor.

Sunshine played to his easy smile. "This is all a mix-up," she told him. "My friend is trying out for a part in a play. She thought you were the director. It could happen to anyone, right?"

Aine finally surveyed him. "I see your great-great-grandfather's look about you. Yer a handsome rogue just like him."

He laughed. "If it was up to me, I'd give her the part. She's totally believable."

"Hear that, Aine?" Sunshine smiled and tried to draw her to her feet. "He says you're good. Let's see if we can find the real director, huh? We'll let these nice people get on with their lunches."

Sean smiled at Aine. "Brava! You're a wonderful actress. I hope to see you in a movie one day."

"Why can't you see who I am?" she asked him in an anguished tone. "You should immediately recognize me as I have known you."

"I'm sorry," he said. "Have we met before?"

"You know these women, Sean?" His companion was beginning to sound neglected and suspicious.

"No, Elena. I've never seen either of them before."

"That's okay." Sunshine left him a business card. "We're leaving now, right, Aine?"

Devastated and unsure what to do, Aine went quietly with her. Had the same enchantment that had made her sleep for so long robbed him of his memory too? He should have instinctively known who she was, even if his forebear hadn't told him.

When they got back to their table, Sunshine asked the waitress to wrap everything up, and they'd take it with them. "We're not quite ready to be in public," she told Jane.

"That's okay. I like to eat at home better anyway."

Aine went with them without raising a word of protest, but outside as they walked back to the office, her appearance changed back to that of the bony gray hag. Jane scooted away from her to walk on the other side of Sunshine.

Glad to be off the street and out of the public eye, Sunshine collapsed in her purple office chair as they got back to the detective agency. Jane scurried to divide the pizza three ways. What was Mr. Bad thinking wanting to add Aine to their employee roster?

Yes, she was powerful—probably more than Sunshine realized. But she was also disturbed and obviously had no idea how to act in society. It had taken them years to be accepted in this community. Aine might blow it all for them.

But she didn't ask him. Instead she sat at her desk and ate her pizza sticks. Aine sat across from her, staring out the window. It was incredibly unnerving for the witch, though she wouldn't have admitted it. Those empty eye sockets and grotesque face weren't something anyone would want to see as they ate.

Sunshine knew she was going to have to take control of the situation. If Mr. Bad wanted the banshee there, he had a good reason. She'd learned not to second guess the rare times he'd had something to say to John. She was going to have to figure out what to do with Aine.

"Are you sure you don't want some of this?" she asked for the third time. There was no response from the banshee. "If not, maybe we should just go ahead and get down to work finding John's killer."

Aine didn't speak or glance her way. Sunshine pulled out John's file. Looking at the photos of him—alive and dead—made something inside her feel dead too.

"You had feelings for the wolf." Aine's voice was like rustling leaves.

"Yes." Sunshine cleared her throat and fought to control her emotions. There was no chance for the vengeance she was seeking if she took the time to mourn him now. First the killer and then the tears. "But they won't get in the way."

Finally Aine turned dead eyes to her. "How do you hold back emotions? How do you force yourself not to cry?"

At first Sunshine thought the banshee was making fun of her. She bristled. But before she could lash out at the hag, Sunshine saw a tear slide down the bony gray face. She meant it. Aine was suffering because her O'Neill wouldn't acknowledge her. She might not be up on all the banshee folklore she needed to work with one of them, but she knew what another soul in pain looked like.

"I loved John with all my heart. I wanted us to be together forever. Now that he's been taken from me, all I can think about is killing whoever took him. I won't let myself fall apart until that's done. That's how I do it—because I have to. It's the last thing I can do for him. Nothing is going to stop me."

The softer, human change came over Aine again. Her fierce, green eyes stared back into Sunshine's suffering gaze. "I understand. This was done to me as well. Sean O'Neill has had his birthright stripped from him. You are right, witch. Nothing else matters until I find out who is responsible and make O'Neill realize who he is and who I am."

"I'll help you with that," Sunshine quickly said. "But I need your help to find John's killer too. Can we agree to that—without the contract?"

"Will he allow it?" Aine jerked her head toward the open door to indicate Mr. Bad.

"I run the business. It's unusual for him to say anything about it." Sunshine smiled. "I really think he just wanted to make sure that you stayed."

"He is a wise and powerful man." Aine considered the agreement that she had been tricked into. "I can agree to help you if you help me."

"Great!" Sunshine was happy to hear it. "Only one more thing—please call me Sunshine or Sunny or anything but witch. Okay?"

"I shall not call you witch again, though I find it difficult to imagine your mother and father naming you Sunshine."

"That's a whole other story. I was thinking we could go to the place where John was killed and see if you get any impressions from it. His death was heavily covered by magic that distracts my own. I know you can follow magic as well as blood. Maybe you can get something there that I couldn't."

Aine was amazed that Sunshine knew about the *beane sidhe*. "How came you to such knowledge, witch—Sunshine? My apologies."

"That's okay. I appreciate the effort." Sunshine got up from her desk and grabbed her handbag. "Actually, there's quite a lot of information about banshees if you know where to look. You have to stay away from the gaming information. Those people are looking for the kind of banshees they need to win."

"Gaming *beane sidhe*?" Aine followed her out of the office. "These are *beane sidhe* who do penance for their crimes by playing games with the families they serve?"

"Not exactly. I'll explain in the car." Sunshine smiled at Jane, who was licking her hands clean of pizza. "Not in public, please. Take messages if anyone calls or stops by. Stay out of the cereal. We'll be back as soon as we can."

"Sure." Jane put her hands in her pockets.

"Car?" Aine asked.

"A carriage without horses," Sunshine explained as they walked into the parking lot that was shaded by dozens of mimosa trees. "It travels very fast, although probably not as fast as you can fly."

"I see." Aine smoothed her hand over the purple convertible as Sunshine opened the doors. "And you do not fly?"

Sunshine laughed. "I've been known to hike up my skirts on a broomstick or two in my time. But mostly I like my car, and it takes too much energy to fly. Get in."

Aine hesitantly got in the car and closed the door behind her. Sunshine started the loud engine that surprised her with its ferocity. No horses—except those from hell—would ever make such sounds.

"Buckle up," Sunshine advised as she held out the seatbelt. "And don't worry, you'll get used to it."

She urged the car forward and out of the parking lot into the street. They got stuck in traffic once, but mostly the roads were clear to the mall where John had been killed.

"I would enjoy owning one of these devices." Aine had a smile on her face. "It goes quite fast. No wonder you discarded the horses. Are all these other cars the same or only yours? Is it magic?"

"Nothing magic about this. Just good old fashioned know-how from Henry Ford." She parked beside two large, blue dumpsters at the back of the mall.

"This is where your lover was killed." Aine's voice was deep and serious.

"Yes." Sunshine got out of the car and stood next to a large bloodstain on the pavement. The dumpster was covered in blood spatter. "John was a powerful werewolf. He knew what he was doing. Yet someone managed to catch him off-guard while he was a wolf. He was ripped to pieces, nearly shredded. I found him here, still in his wolf state, despite his death."

Aine crouched close to the blacktop and touched her finger to the dried blood. She inhaled of it deeply and then stuck it in her mouth.

Sunshine looked away before she gagged. She hadn't expected something so visceral from the banshee. She really needed to look up more information about her.

"Yes," Aine said. "There was definitely magic covering this death. Whoever killed him was a strong, fast predator. Probably not one of your breed."

"You mean not a witch," Sunshine said when she could control herself. "What then? There aren't many creatures that can destroy a werewolf that way."

"Perhaps another wolf."

"I thought of that. Do you smell anything of another wolf here? I tried a spell that should have shown me if a wolf killed John. There was nothing."

Aine's jaws creaked as they moved while she rolled the taste of blood around in her mouth. "I cannot say—which is odd. Is there anything else I should see while we're here?"

"I think these dents in the metal were made by the attacker pushing John's head into them."

"No. I don't think so." Aine put her hand in each of the dozen or so dents. "This was done by the attacker out of rage. He was hard put to kill the wolf, and it inflamed him. He used his fists to express that anger."

Sunshine forced herself to control her emotions. She swallowed hard and looked away. "Anything else from that?"

"Behold my fist in this indentation." Aine kept her hand there. It fit into the dent, but the shape was unique. "The attacker had clawed hands to make such a mark. It is another sign of his strength, yet he did not best the wolf easily. The fight was dreadful. The wolf depleted his strength. Have you searched for a creature with injuries such as these that had been inflicted during the battle?"

"There are a lot of people in Norfolk," Sunshine said. "It would be hard to find one large person with injuries unless we had help from the police. Would you know his scent?"

Aine sniffed her hand, the ground, and the dumpster. "I believe I would know it, yes. Do you recognize the magic done here?"

"No. I wish I did. I always thought every witch left a

signature. But either this wasn't a witch or she's very good."

"I don't believe a witch killed a wolf—not in this manner. Do you?"

"No. But I don't know what it was. And that bothers both me and Mr. Bad."

They walked around the corner of the dumpster and the O'Neill heir was waiting for them.

"Detective Sean O'Neill." He flashed his badge. "Were you two spying on me at the pizzeria? What do you know about the murder that took place here?"

Jane scurried to divide the pizza three ways.

Chapter Four

"Spying?" Sunshine's hair crackled with energy. "I don't think so."

"It seems strange that you were there with your 'actress' friend and now you're here."

In any other situation, Sunshine might have considered him attractive and interesting but not now. "We heard about the murder." She shrugged, hoping Aine could hold it together. "We came to see what the crime scene looked like. Sorry."

"Okay. Let's see some ID." He put his hand out. "And I want to know what you're really doing here."

Aine put her hands over her face. It was difficult to control her emotions around him. It was taking its toll on her. She wasn't sure how much longer she could keep the human face she'd donned.

"You too." O'Neill glanced at her. "Let's see some ID."

"She doesn't have any," Sunshine said. "She has

amnesia that might be connected with this case."

"Case? Amnesia?" He checked Sunshine's ID. "You're a private detective? Is that right?"

"Yes. And she's my client."

"And how is it related to this investigation?"

"I don't know yet." She was beginning to lose steam. She could use magic on him, but she had a feeling Aine would take exception to that. The aftermath could be an ugly contest between them.

"Maybe you should let me help you with her problem, Miss Merryweather." He handed her ID back. "This is a police matter. If she's involved, we should know. Let's take a ride, shall we?"

Detective O'Neill allowed them to go to the downtown station in Sunshine's convertible after she'd begged him on Aine's behalf. He agreed but followed them there in his car, accompanied by a female detective.

"Are you okay?" Sunshine asked Aine when they were alone. "Can you handle this?"

She turned a face that was half hag to her. "I am not 'okay.' I do not understand any of this. I need to make contact with him. He needs to acknowledge me."

"So you completely fall apart when you see him." Sunshine nodded. "Don't worry. I've dated men like that before. But we have to do something about this. If you want to impress this O'Neill with who and what you are to him, you can't turn into ice cream and melt at the sight of him."

"I do not understand your words. Ice cream? What is this? How do I avoid it?"

Sunshine stopped the car outside the police station. "I could try putting a spell on you so you recognize him but keep your bearing."

"I could still be in the thrall of the enchantment that made me sleep for two centuries. I dare not risk losing any further time. When he is departed from this world, I go too. My only hope of fulfilling my pledge to this family is to see him wed and his wife fat with child."

"I don't see the sweet thing at the pizzeria getting fat with anything." Sunshine considered the situation. "But that doesn't mean they can't produce an heir together."

"There must be some way to make him understand." Aine came as close to fretting over the problem as it was possible for one who had witnessed the horrors of the grave.

"What would it have been like in your time, before you went to sleep?"

"I would have waited until the heir reached puberty and entered his first man-dream as his *beane sidhe*. He would have been warned as a child to expect me. There would have been fear, but also gladness that I would predict his death so he could prepare."

"Okay." Sunshine rolled the idea around in her head as Aine had rolled the blood around in her mouth. Her hair swirled around her as she considered what to do next. "So he needs to go to sleep and have a wet dream. I think that's what you're saying."

Aine nodded. "But he is well past his childhood."

"Not a problem. After all, it only starts then, right? You can get him used to the idea at any time. Hang in there. Let me handle this. Don't say anything inside. I'll explain my plan when we're finished."

Aine accompanied Sunshine into the office with her head down. She was able to control her appearance but was still drawn to O'Neill. She had to keep herself facing away from him. This wasn't the place to attempt to explain everything. She reminded herself that, without his recognition, they could have no meaningful relationship. He had to understand who she was and what she could bring to him.

Police officers in uniform walked by them as they brought in new arrests. Detective O'Neill was courteous as he accompanied them inside and seated them at a small, metal table in a private room. He offered coffee, but

Sunshine declined for them both.

Finally he sat opposite them. Aine clung to Sunshine's side as though she couldn't leave it and stared at the floor.

"Look, I'm not arresting you. I just want to find out what you know about the murder of John Lancaster." He took out a pad of paper. "First of all, was that his real name? What else can you tell me about him? He didn't have a job or a Social Security number. I can't find a birth certificate."

"Has your medical examiner had a chance to look at the body? Does he know what killed him?" Sunshine felt as though they'd both fired warning shots at each other. Now they'd get down to the real battle.

"If you'd seen the crime scene before it was taken care of, you'd know there wasn't much of Mr. Lancaster left to ID. There was probably DNA, of course, but it's too soon for that. We were fortunate to be able to use his teeth to figure out who he was. As for what killed him, we don't know yet. I was hoping maybe you could tell us."

Sunshine knew that John Lancaster wasn't John's real name. Like many other werewolves and creatures that lived outside society, he regularly changed his name. A werewolf couldn't be too careful. "I wish I could help, but I don't know what killed John."

"Were you friends with Mr. Lancaster?" he probed. "Lovers?"

"He and I were work associates."

"At the detective agency? Is that what he did for a living?" O'Neill wrote what she said.

"When I first met him, he was a salesman for a silver company." That had made her laugh when he'd first told her. She'd known what he was when she met him. The irony of him selling one of the few things that could kill him hadn't missed her.

O'Neill filled in that information and glanced at Aine. "How does she fit in? Was she his girlfriend? Did she hire you to find him?"

"Actually that's exactly what happened." Sunshine gladly snapped up his explanation. "She came here looking for him and hired me to help her find him."

"So she could be involved in his death?"

"No. She was with me when it happened. We were also with several other people, if you need their names."

"Yes. I'll need those names. I know she speaks, Miss Merryweather. I heard her at the restaurant. I'd like to hear her side of the story."

"I'd like to help you with that, but she's been traumatized. She didn't even recognize John at first. She's been to the hospital, but they can't find anything physically wrong with her. The doctor said it could take time."

"Okay." He wrote down what she told him, but the expression on his face said he wasn't happy with it.

Aine wanted to explain, but she knew it would only come out as babble. She listened carefully but had no idea what Sunshine was talking about.

He glanced at them and shook his head. "Look. I'm going to be honest with you. I haven't had this job for long. I need a good CI to help with information from the street on this, and maybe other cases. Maybe you could be that person, Sunshine."

He certainly has a winning smile. "I can help where possible," she said. "But there's the matter of confidentiality between me and my clients, including Mr. Lancaster."

"He's dead," he reminded her. "I think that ends when your client passes."

"Except in this case where my new client could also be in danger."

"All right. I have no reason to keep you. But if she gets her memory back, I need to know. If you hear anything that might help us find Mr. Lancaster's killer, I'd appreciate a call." He put a business card on the table before her. "Thanks for coming in."

Sunshine grabbed it and got to her feet, one arm around

Aine as though she was supporting her.

As they were leaving, a short, tough-looking brunette walked in. She had a detective's badge pinned to her side—O'Neill's partner.

Aine didn't move away from Sunshine's protective grasp as they walked quickly outside to the convertible. "Is it over? What will happen now?"

"Get in the car. Now's not a good time to talk. Did you see the look in O'Neill's partner's eyes? She's not finished with us. I think we may be their only lead on John's death. Let's not ruffle her feathers."

"You mean you think she may try to harm him?" Aine demanded as she got in. "I won't allow that. It is not his time to die."

"That's not what I mean." Sunshine got behind the steering wheel. "Right now, we need some space to figure this out. We can't do that if she's all over us or if you're in a mental hospital because they can't figure out what you are."

Aine blinked. "I cannot be held against my will if that is what worries you."

"How close are you usually with the O'Neill heirs?"

"I have had deep friendships with many of the O'Neills. They have valued my advice and wisdom. Our bond is personal and deep."

Sunshine's hair appeared as though it might fly away at any moment. She smoothed it down, straightened her purple dress, and kept driving. "Let's not worry about it right now. I'm sure I can find a spell to handle this problem."

"Do not presume to work your magic on him," Aine warned. "I would defend O'Neill with mighty force if necessary."

Just what I thought you'd say. "Take it easy. I'm not going to do anything to him. I was talking about you. Your relationship with him is all screwed up right now. How can you interact with him if you can't look at him or talk to him without losing it?"

"Yes. You have the right of it," Aine admitted in a shamed voice.

"We'll see. You might be more than a spell can handle, although it sounds as though someone put a spell on you and kept you asleep for longer than you should've been."

"Ten O'Neills went to their graves without my cries to warn them, without me beside them going to the underworld. It is a dark stain against me."

"But there's not a scorekeeper besides you either," Sunshine reminded her. "Everything you suffer from your past is because you believe you deserve it. Besides being under a spell that kept you from your designated tasks with the O'Neills, what have you ever done that was so terrible?"

"I murdered fourteen O'Neills as they lay sleeping in their beds. I did this for a false lover who used me to further his ambition. Then as I learned of his treachery, I murdered him and every member of his line so his seed would not survive on this earth."

Sunshine parked the car in the parking lot at the detective agency. "Oh. Well, I guess that's a lot then, isn't it? And that's why you serve the O'Neills—to make up for everything. What about your lover's family?"

"Because he spoke lies to me, I was pardoned for his death. His family line naturally would be part of that."

"Naturally." Sunshine got out of the car. "Things were much different back then. Now we just kill one or two at a time and go to jail. Except for John's killer. When I find him, I'm going to make sure there isn't enough left of him to put in jail."

Aine understood. "We are similar in nature. Are you prepared to face whatever judgment comes to you from your actions?"

"I am." For a moment her blue eyes hardened into unbreakable sapphires. Her soft jaw was tough, and an expression came over her pretty face that promised horrors for her lover's killer.

Then her face changed again, and she was as good-natured as ever. Aine considered that Sunshine's family should have given her two names to accommodate her dual nature. Aine's appearance might change, but she always remained the same inside—proud, vengeful, and strong.

They went in the old building. Jane jumped up from the front desk at their appearance.

"It's been real quiet," she told her boss. "Maybe everyone knows you're searching for John's killer."

Sunshine's answering smile didn't reach her eyes. "Since we don't have any foot traffic right now, Aine—probably good since we're concentrated on you and John—why don't we get you settled upstairs? We can start working on both cases after. How does that sound?"

"I don't understand. What are we settling?"

Sunshine closed her eyes to seek patience. "Didn't I mention that Jane and I live upstairs? I thought I did. There's plenty of room for you too. There used to be a boarding house here before I bought the place. We live upstairs and work down here. It's very convenient and a good tax write-off."

"Mr. Bad lives with this arrangement?"

"No. Actually Mr. Bad lives and works down here. He doesn't leave his office."

"He uses a false name to protect his identity. Do you not wish to know who he really is?"

"I really don't. He's Mr. Bad, and that's enough for me. I'm going to set up a room for Aine," she told Jane. "Take messages, please. And try not to nibble on them."

"May I be myself unless someone comes in or the phone rings?" Jane asked.

"Of course. Everyone needs some me time. We'll be down in a while."

Sunshine pushed a button in the wall, and an elevator appeared. "There was no elevator in the building when I bought it. I left the stairs in but created this for quick getaways if necessary."

"You mean this el-e-va-tor was created by magic." The word was strange to her, but what was not in this time? Aine looked at the inside of the box she'd stepped into. "Impressive. You are a witch of rare abilities."

"Thanks." The purple elevator closed when they were inside. "It was more a matter of convenience but also saved me a butt-load of money. Even fifty years ago, elevators were expensive."

In the proverbial blink of an eye, the elevator had reached the second floor.

"Jane and I share this floor. You're welcome to have the spare bedroom. For those times you just want to wail, there are two floors up from this one. They aren't as well cared for, but a few times a year I send in a mop and broom. I don't want a lot of dust to build up in case I need the extra space in a hurry."

Naturally the floor where they walked was heavy in purple wall accents and furniture.

"Why do you keep this mouse-woman here with you?" Aine asked.

"We all make mistakes," Sunshine said. "You were right. Jane is one of mine."

"How so?"

"It was early on when I first came into my power. I was trying to make everything better with magic." Sunshine shrugged as she opened a door into a large bedroom and sitting area. "There was a robbery at a convenience store where I was waiting in line. I saw the thief's gun and threw some magic at it. It stopped the robbery, and no one else was even aware that it had happened—except for Jane. My magic killed her family and somehow made her a shapeshifter. But she's more a mouse that can become a human than John was a human who could become a wolf."

Aine took in all the fine, expensive rugs, and the drapes on the big window near the bed. Like everything here, it was the best money could buy. Sunshine took great pride in her home and accomplishments. In the banshee's time, even a king and queen would not have lived with such splendor and finery.

"And you keep her with you because you owe a debt. I understand," Aine said. "This room is very pleasurable to the eye."

"I'm so glad you like it. Some people don't like purple as much as I do."

"But it is the color of royalty," Aine said. "Who could not feel regal sleeping here?"

Sunshine's cell phone rang. It was Jane with a warning.

"I have to handle something that's come up. You can stay up here and get some rest. We can talk later."

"I have been dead for centuries. Repose holds no fascination for me. I shall come with you. Perhaps you might need my assistance."

Sunshine was about to deny that she needed any help from Aine when someone bellowed her name loudly enough to shake the foundations of the building.

"That wasn't Mr. Bad."

"No. On second thought, maybe you should come with me."

Chapter Five

They went down in the elevator to find Jane cowering in a corner. She was too terrified to take human form.

Standing in front of her was a large man whose presence dominated the room. He was wearing a blood red suit with a matching hat. His skin was coarse and a lighter shade than his clothing. He was tall—at least seven feet—with thick arms and legs.

"There you are." His tone was refined in the smaller space, with none of the power that he'd exhibited calling to her. "I was wondering what it takes to get your attention these days, Miss Merryweather."

"So you decided to scream at me and crack a few bricks," she countered. "What do you want, Caeford?"

"You and I have a deal. You handle my loose ends. My ends are loose, Miss Merryweather. They aren't being handled."

"Let me introduce you to our new associate. This is

Aine. She'll be taking over John's position. You know we've been understaffed. Things will get back to normal now."

Yellow eyes surveyed Aine with distaste. "She's not a wolf." He sniffed. "What is she?"

"Aine is a banshee," Sunshine said. "I guarantee she'll do everything John did and more once she's trained."

"A *beane sidhe*? Really? I thought they'd died out centuries ago. Interesting."

"It appears not. What loose ends are you looking to tie up right now, Caeford?" Sunshine asked.

"A man saw me change last week on a rooftop downtown. He hasn't said anything yet, but I need to be sure of his silence. Otherwise I'll have to take care of it myself." He was still staring at Aine.

"Of course. We'll take care of it right away," Sunshine said with a smile. "I'll send you a text when it's done."

"Good. I won't have to take my business elsewhere." He sniffed at Aine one last time before he gave Sunshine the address and turned to leave the building. A large gold-headed cane was in his meaty right hand.

When he was gone, Sunshine spoke to Jane in gentle, low tones. She convinced the mouse to go upstairs and lie down. The tiny creature scampered up the stairs.

"She doesn't like the elevator," Sunshine explained.

"What of the dragon?" Aine asked. "What hold has he over you?"

Sunshine laughed and went into her office to sit down. "Hold? Not a hold, unless you count two thousand dollars a month in gold. It's really more a retainer. Caeford likes to get drunk sometimes and causes trouble that he expects us to clean up for him. How did you know he was a dragon? Even John didn't know until I told him."

"I've met dragons. They have a look about them even if they are in human form. What do you plan to do to take care of the man who saw him change? Will you kill him?"

"No. We don't kill people for our clients. John used to

have a talk with the poor bystander and convince him or her that he was even scarier than the dragon. I'll probably use magic."

"But you would like me to do this for you as part of my employment here," Aine stated.

"Possibly. But that would be later when you've had some sensitivity training. You can't go in there screaming or using other banshee magic that would draw attention. We have twenty-four hour news that picks up on the crazy things and cell phone cameras that can take pictures of everything. Our clients rely on our discretion."

"Much of what you say makes no sense to me, but I am trying to learn. There is no other life for me to go back to. I need to understand this one if I am going to be of counsel to the O'Neill family."

"Great. We could probably take care of Caeford's little problem before dinner and come back to decide our next move in John's investigation." Sunshine peered into Aine's worn, but very human, face. "Do you think you can hold on to this now? Like I said, the idea is to make everything as normal looking as we can."

Aine nodded. "I have my triple forms under control for the moment. Only with O'Neill do I seem to have difficulty."

"And we'll work on that spell when we get back. I don't want Caeford to withdraw his support. He was one of my first clients, and is a good friend of Mr. Bad." They started out of the office together and Sunshine paused. "Three forms? What's the third one?"

Aine's face and form changed from the middle-aged human in black to a young, vibrant woman with bright red hair flowing down her back. She had brilliant green eyes, and her gown was rich, green velvet with a gold and jeweled girdle about her slender hips. "Thus you see me as I was when a young Queen of Ulster. I have rarely taken this shape in the last hundred years. There is too much pain in the reminder of who I was and who I am."

"Wow. You should've looked like this when we talked to O'Neill." Sunshine winked at her. "That would have gotten his attention."

"But not the attention I need from him," Aine said as they left.

"No. Of course not. I was joking with you. They had joking back a few hundred years ago, right?"

"Of course." Aine reverted to her middle-aged form in black. "I had many jesters when I was queen and saw many more in the O'Neill castle. This is not a new concept to me."

"Good. Because you could lighten up some. Everything isn't a matter of life and death. Smile once in a while. It won't break your face."

Aine tried a smile at Sunshine's request. It was difficult and resembled a grimace more than a smile.

"Work on it. My mother always told me that you catch more flies with honey than with vinegar."

Not sure how that applied to her present circumstance, Aine followed Sunshine down the sidewalk. The building where the dragon had transformed in the sight of an unknowing human was close to the detective agency.

The two women went in the multi-storied building and took an elevator to the top. This elevator was different, Aine found, and not controlled by magic. There was a powerful thrust and whirring sound as it moved slowly to its destination.

The rooftop was another short flight of stairs from the floor where the elevator had left them.

"Why would this human remain here after seeing something as terrifying as a dragon unfurling his wings to glide across the city?" Aine asked.

"It's human nature to stay in the same area," Sunshine explained as she cast a spell to search out the man who'd witnessed Caeford's transformation. "He may not be up here right now. Or he may work here. We need a clue about who he is and where we can find him. My spell should take care of it."

While the remainder of the rooftop still appeared in normal shades of gray and dirty white, one spot gleamed like a beacon when the spell fell on it.

"And there he is!" Sunshine announced. "This won't take long at all."

They rounded a large air conditioning unit and almost walked right into a group of police officers.

"What the—?" Sunshine said too loudly.

Detective O'Neill's partner stepped in front of them. "Well looky here, Sean. Aren't these the same two women from the other murder?"

O'Neill had been hidden from them by an old smokestack. "Ladies. Another coincidence?"

They went down in the elevator to find Jane cowering in a corner. She was too terrified to take human form.

Chapter Six

O'Neill's partner was named Sharon Malto. She was a short, angry woman with lines of defiance etched throughout her body. Her dark brown eyes narrowed as she studied Sunshine and Aine.

"I don't think this is a coincidence," she told O'Neill. "What are the chances that they'd turn up at two similar crime scenes—this one where the victim is hardly even cold. I think we should arrest them and look into who and what they are."

Aine managed to hold herself together and looked past O'Neill and his partner. The police were trying to cover a huge crime scene where yet another victim had been torn to pieces. Blood was everywhere. They could cover the rooftop, but red still dripped from the smokestack and the air conditioning unit.

"That's very amusing," Sunshine said. "But if we'd killed this person, I think we'd be covered in blood too, don't you, Detective O'Neill?"

"Unless you went home to change and came back," he said. "Let's pull out the UV light and run it across them. No matter how well you clean up, there's bound to be some blood left behind."

One of the crime scene techs was called over. The detectives escorted Sunshine and Aine back into the building to a darkened area where the UV light could work its magic.

Detective Malto wasn't pleased when not even a single

hair on either woman's head showed blood in the light. They checked their clothes, the bottom of their shoes, not to mention their hands and fingernails. There was no sign that they had been at the murder.

Back on the roof again, Detective O'Neill asked why they were there.

"We're investigating a case for a client," Sunshine told him. "You know that. We didn't know about the murder. It just happened that way."

"And what exactly are you investigating now, Ms. Merryweather?" Detective Malto wondered. "We need the name of the client who sent you here and his part in this."

Aine faced her accuser. She'd known powerless women such as this one during her long life. "Our client has no part in this unfortunate happening. And our cases are our own."

"I guess she got her memory back," O'Neill remarked. "How are you feeling this afternoon?"

The last was asked of Aine. She took one look at him, gulped, and tried to stand her ground. She tried to forget what she owed him and his family. She remembered who she was and who she had been.

"I am feeling quite well this afternoon, thank you, O'Neill." Her face was a frozen mask. She refused to allow her inner turmoil to show. "We would both no doubt like to help you with this situation, but alas, we are unable."

"Nice." He gestured to Sunshine. "Would you mind coming over here a minute, Ms. Merryweather? I need a word with you."

Aine stayed where she was with the short, angry female detective as Sunshine accompanied O'Neill to the other side of the large smoke stack.

"What's going on?" he asked in a quiet voice. "All that stuff you told me about her wasn't true, was it?"

"As far as I knew at that time, it was true." Did she dare use a charm spell on him? Maybe Aine wouldn't notice. "That's the way amnesia works. One minute they don't know who they are, and the next they know everything."

"And you also decided to hire her to be your spokesperson?"

"No. I hired her to keep her close at hand. Her life could be in danger. I thought this way was best."

"Fine. I want to interview her about the Lancaster murder since you said she knew him."

Sunshine knew she needed a way out of this maze she'd made for herself. "All right. She's not one hundred percent yet, but I'm sure she'll be glad to speak with you."

"I'll take what I can get. I want to talk to both of you about this second murder. It seems too much like the first to think it wasn't done by the same person."

"I was considering exactly the same thing. We're on the same wavelength, Detective O'Neill. I'm sure we can solve these unfortunate circumstances together before anything else happens."

"I want to see you in my office in an hour, Ms. Merryweather. Don't make me find you."

"Don't worry about it. We'll be there."

They rejoined and interrupted the staring match between Detective Malto and Aine. Sunshine suggested she and Aine should leave the roof. Detective Malto turned to her partner to ask what he was thinking letting them go.

"And on that note," Sunshine said. "Let's get out of here."

"Whilst you were speaking with O'Neill," Aine said, "I smelled the same odor as from the other murder. Whoever killed this man killed your wolf as well."

"You're thinking it was Caeford, aren't you?" Sunshine asked as they got back in the elevator.

"It would make sense. The dragon wanted to throw suspicion on to us so he wouldn't be caught in it."

"He would never do such a thing," Sunshine told her. "I'm not saying he wouldn't hire someone to do it, but that dragon is too clever to get blood on his hands."

"Perhaps he hired another then," Aine suggested. "We should speak with him on the matter."

"The police couldn't touch him." Sunshine's brain was working a mile a minute. Something more was going on. She didn't believe the ancient dragon killed John or this man. There was another answer.

"I myself have killed a dragon," Aine said conversationally. "It is difficult but not impossible."

Sunshine grabbed her arm as they reached the bottom floor of the building. "Let's not talk about this right now. You! You actually talked to Detective O'Neill without turning into sponge cake. Congratulations. You found a way to handle it."

"Why do you find food references to be so useful?" Aine asked. "There was no danger that I would be reduced to any of the food you've mentioned."

"Yes, but I wasn't sure you'd be able to look him in the eyes." Sunshine was happy to see the change in her companion. "And he has such pretty eyes, don't you think?"

Aine blinked. "His eyes have nothing to do with our relationship. The O'Neills have always been tall, straight, and handsome."

"Come on." Sunshine opened the door, and they walked back out into the waning afternoon. "It's okay to think he's good-looking. You can still haunt him—although I have a feeling you'd be haunting him and Detective Malto too. Did you see the way she looked at him? There's something hot and heavy going on there. I wonder if the woman from the pizzeria knows about them."

"I shall hope one of them bears him many children."

"Good enough. I think we can do without that spell to help you. You appear to have found your banshee legs. You just needed some time to adjust. You're going to be fine."

"Thank you—although my legs have never been in question." Aine wondered if everyone in this time spoke like Sunshine. "What about the dragon? Do we hunt him or allow the police to do so? I do not believe O'Neill could handle the beast."

"Handle it? O'Neill would never believe it. Let me discuss this with Mr. Bad. He might have some answers, and I'll know how to approach Caeford. In the meantime, you get settled in your room. If you need anything, let me know. I know you have a lot to adjust to. I'll be happy to help in any way I can."

Aine felt she had long since passed the time of pleasantries in her life. It was a surprise to find she had not. She enjoyed the witch's banter and her kindness. Though she was only there for O'Neill, it was sweet to feel her warmth. It filled her as the sun had once done when she was alive.

After seeing Aine to the elevator, Sunshine went immediately to speak with Mr. Bad. He could be moody and difficult about small things, according to John. She hoped that wouldn't be the case in speaking of the dragon. While Aine might be convinced a dragon could be killed, Sunshine had never known anyone to do such a thing. Fortunately for mankind, the few dragons left on earth had learned to disguise themselves and used cunning to survive instead of the flame.

She didn't want to imagine that those times were going to change.

Sunshine knocked on Mr. Bad's office door. He called for her to come in. As usual the room was in heavy shadow. She could make out his form at the desk but no details.

She'd lied to Aine when she'd told her she wasn't curious about him. She wondered from the moment she'd met him who and what he was. But no amount of witchery, carefully applied, had brought those answers to her. She didn't want to risk losing his support enough to peer deeper.

"Yes." His voice was exhaled on a hoarse breath.

"You know why I'm here." She sat in a chair near the door. She'd never been closer to him than this.

"Yes."

"Did he mislead us? Did he kill John and the man who saw him on the rooftop? Because Aine and I agree that it was the same person who did both deeds. We both think—"

"I know what you suppose."

"And?"

"I agree with you. The same person committed both murders."

"Was that Caeford? I can't believe he'd rip someone apart that way and not use his flame to cover it up. It would only take a single blast to destroy the evidence left behind."

"It seems you have your answer."

"And yet he's the one who led us to the new murder."

"So it appears."

She got to her feet. "Thank you. Please let me know if you have any further insight." She was a little put out by his lack of answers to the problem.

"Miss Merryweather?" He stopped her from leaving. "Sometimes insight is simply more questions that haven't been answered."

"I suppose that's true. Aine and I are beginning to get along. I think you were right and she could be a valuable ally."

"Yes."

She knew their conversation was over when he didn't speak again. Possibly from Aine's challenge to know him better, she tiptoed toward his desk. The dark seemed to be deeper here, as though it was working to hide him from her. She leaned toward him, hoping to catch just a glimpse.

"Was there something else?" His voice was deep and strong, sounding as though he was right beside her when she could see his outline in the chair.

Not a nervous person by nature, still she gasped in surprise. "No. That's it. Aine and I have to meet with the police again. Detective O'Neill may be the man she wants to be close to, but he's a little too insistent for my taste."

There was no response. This time, Sunshine walked to

the door, closing it firmly behind her as she left his room.

What was she doing? What was she thinking? Mr. Bad needed his privacy. She'd always respected that need. She had plenty of other things to look into, especially if Caeford wasn't the killer and yet now was involved in the murder.

She wouldn't mention that to Detective O'Neill or his bulldog-like partner, Detective Malto, but she knew it was true. They wouldn't know they were dealing with a dragon. Even if they somehow realized who he was and brought him in for questioning, no jail could hold him.

Sunshine put her mind to thinking about anything else the two murders might have in common. That task was over quickly since she couldn't imagine anything.

"Jane? Are you here?" she asked.

"Yes. Of course." Jane walked out of the supply closet. "Is there something you'd like me to do?"

"I was wondering if you could dig up some information about the man who was just killed on the roof. That might be a great help to me. You're so good with the computer. I need something that might connect John's death to the second man."

"Okay. You know we're almost out of donuts. I'd hate for a client to come in and there would be no donuts to serve."

"I'll be sure to get some while I'm out."

"And some sweet cereal." Jane's nose twitched and her slender fingers moved as though she still had tiny claws.

"That too. Thank you." Her young charge had a deathly fear of any type store. It probably reminded her too much of what had happened. Jane was a big help in many other ways, but she was always hungry.

The front door opened, and Sunshine looked up in surprise to see O'Neill and Detective Malto walk into the agency.

"We were waiting for you at the station," he said. "When you didn't show, we decided to drop by and check out your place."

Detective Malto's brown eyes swept over the abundance of purple in the waiting area. "Not bad if you like purple."

"I do like purple." Sunshine's voice was friendly and warm. "Please have a seat in my office. Aine is resting from her ordeal on the roof. I'll get her. Would you like some coffee or tea?"

"No." O'Neill glanced toward her office. "Don't leave us hanging, Miss Merryweather. We don't want to look for you again."

"I'll be right back," she promised.

As soon as they were in her office, she got in the elevator and went upstairs to get Aine. She knew this was more than just a quick visit for the detectives. They were snooping around, hoping to find something that would close the case for them. She wouldn't let that happen even if it meant using magic on O'Neill and his partner. Aine would have to understand.

Sunshine rapped quickly at the bedroom door. When there was no response, she pushed it open and stared at the empty space.

Aine was gone.

Chapter Seven

Closing her eyes, Sunshine cast a broad spell to search for the banshee. Her concentration was tugged at from all directions making it difficult to maintain the spell. Maybe that was why she couldn't find Aine. The spell should have been able to pinpoint her position within fifty miles. But there was no sign of her.

Now what?

Going back downstairs before the police detectives began looking through the rest of the building, Sunshine conjured as she went. They weren't going to accept that Aine was gone. She had to allay their suspicions and then she could concentrate on finding her new associate.

Creating a magic duplicate of Aine was the only answer she could think of in the time it took the elevator to reach the ground floor. She was going to be drained when it was done, but it would take care of the issue. She could also control Aine's answers to the detective's questions. That would be a plus since the banshee's responses were unreliable.

Sunshine got off the elevator with a smile on her pretty face. Aine's doppelganger was there in her middle aged-form dressed in black. The hag version of her would scare the wits out of them, and the high queen form was over the top.

"Here we are," Sunshine said as she entered the room. She moved magical Aine to a chair in the corner and had her sit but not look at the detectives in her usual, direct manner. "Now what can we do for you?"

The conversation was brief. Sunshine and Aine had ironclad alibis for both murders. They were involved in the case only from the standpoint of representing John Lancaster. They were on the rooftop following a lead in that case that happened to coincide with the second death though they knew nothing about the second victim.

Sunshine was starting to get a headache from the effort of keeping up the appearance that Aine was there. Worse, her magical version of Aine was starting to look blurred at the edges. It wouldn't be long before someone began to question their vision—if they didn't guess that she wasn't real.

Jane burst into the room with an expression of extreme agitation. Her right leg was trembling violently. "Miss Merryweather—there's someone to see you."

"Please tell them I can't be disturbed right now." Sunshine could only imagine that Caeford was waiting for her in the outer office. Now was not the time.

"She insists. And I don't want to upset her with her . . . powerful singing voice." Jane's finely drawn brows lifted.

"Oh." Sunshine got to her feet. So did the magical Aine. "This will only take a moment, detectives. If you'll excuse me."

"Excuse me," the doppelganger said.

"That's all right." O'Neill got to his feet too. Malto stood beside him. "I think we're done here for now, Miss Merryweather. If you think of anything else we should know, give us a call."

"I definitely will. Thank you for coming by. Jane will show you to the door."

Jane started twitching all over and holding her hands in front of her. "I will? Of course I will." This at Sunshine's nod. "This way, detectives. Are you sure you wouldn't like some coffee? I have to-go cups."

While the detectives were focused on Jane, Sunshine let go of the magic version of Aine and opened a portal on the other side from the doorway they were using. She snatched Aine into her office and closed it then sank into a chair, exhausted.

Aine watched O'Neill and his partner leaving the room. "Is there a problem?"

"No. Not now. Where were you? The police came for a visit and you were gone," Sunshine explained.

Aine dropped gracefully into an empty chair. "I fell asleep, I believe, and found myself in O'Neill's home."

"His *home*?" Sunshine hissed, careful of her tone since she could still hear Jane with the detectives as they were leaving the agency. "Why did you go there?"

"My quest will not be denied. I unconsciously went there to contact him." She pushed back the black hood on her cape. "It was not something I did a 'purpose. The bond between us is growing stronger now that I've met him."

"I thought you had that under control?"

"I have control of my appearance. The emotional aspect wasn't one I considered. I must claim my place in his life now. It could be worse if I don't do what I am bound."

"Fine. But you have to stop disappearing, whatever that takes. I had to create an alternate you from magic. The detectives didn't only want to speak to me. Your presence was essential."

"You duplicated me with magic?" Aine raised one brow. Storms of anger raged in her eyes.

"Calm down. It was only like a photograph of you. Just an image projected for the police."

"Photograph?" Aine tried the word in her mouth.

"Painting," Sunshine corrected. "Like a moving, speaking, painting of you."

"That was clever." Aine changed the subject. "I know where O'Neill lives now. I shall enter his dreams tonight. Once we bond and he understands why I'm here, that should take care of any future unexplained disappearances."

"Do what you need to do. The detectives are satisfied with our explanation about the two deaths, at least for now."

"What did Mr. Bad have to say about Caeford?"

"He was his usual noncommittal self. That's the best we're going to get from him right now." Sunshine did her best to conceal her anger and frustration with him.

"It seems it might be best to replace Mr. Bad, despite his power. If he does nothing to help you, perhaps it would be better to find another who might be more responsive."

The banshee didn't understand Sunshine's relationship with the strange man. Not surprising since sometimes she didn't understand it herself. How could she explain that there were those moments when his wisdom made all the difference? Or that many of her clients were his friends?

"Mr. Bad comes in handy, besides paying rent." Sunshine knew Aine would understand and respect that commitment. "He stays no matter what."

"I see. A tale for another time then, eh?"

"Yes. Right now we need to see Caeford and decide if he's telling the truth about his encounter on the roof. I have Jane working on the computer finding out what she can about the man who died there. I can't imagine there could be any tie to John, but it's possible."

"And a computer would be a form of magic?" Aine asked.

"Electronic magic," Sunshine agreed. "Let's go."

"That was too close," Jane stammered as the two women walked out of the inner office. "My digestive system is not handling the stress. Maybe you should include nuts and seeds with the cereal and donuts when you go to the store. Nothing like nuts and seeds to quiet the belly. That's what my mama always told us."

Aine and Sunshine watched her rub her stomach.

"I'll put that on the list," Sunshine promised. "Have you learned anything about the dead man on the roof?"

Jane read what she had on the computer monitor. "His name was Harley Matthews. He was thirty-two years old. Born and raised in Norfolk. He worked at a tattoo place over on Third Street, *Tattoo Hell*."

Sunshine filed away that information. "Thanks. Keep digging, will you? We'll be back after we see Caeford."

Aine followed her to the car. "What magic that box has in it! The wonders of your time are very impressive."

"Sometimes," Sunshine agreed as she got in the car. "Sometimes I'm sure the old ways were better. No traffic jams. No police detectives—or you could get rid of them. There are a lot of handicaps put on witches today to keep real magic off CNN."

Aine puzzled over that. "CNN?"

"That's another one for later. Strap in. Let's get this over with."

Caeford lived in a deep sub-basement in the heart of the city. Sunshine parked the car at the curb outside the office building structure. It looked like any other older building from the fifties. No one would ever guess that a dragon lived here amidst the steel, concrete, and glass.

"This time we take the elevator as far down as we can and then the stairs," Sunshine told Aine.

They were packed into a crowded elevator filled with men and women in suits carrying briefcases. Soft music played in the background as the arrival of each floor was heralded by a chime. No one spoke, searching instead on their handheld devices.

When they were finally alone for the basement floor, Aine spoke. She was starting to understand the secrecy of this time. "A good place for a dragon to dwell. But he unfurled his wings at a spot distant from this. He, too, must remain unseen in this place."

"We all do—all magical creatures. It's something we've learned."

"It wasn't that different during my time. Witches were frequently hunted and killed, especially those with no real power. Dragons were hunted to extinction for sport and the use of their body parts. It was the same with unicorns and other creatures. But perhaps if it were not so, this city you live in wouldn't exist."

"I guess there are good and bad things about each time in history," Sunshine acknowledged. "Except for toilets. I never want to use a toilet in the woods—no holes in the ground with rude buildings over them. I like my toilets inside with water and flush boxes."

Aine smiled.

"What? Don't banshees use a toilet?"

"Hardly. We are dead, after all. We do not eat, so we do not excrete."

"Good to know. I'm saving up banshee facts for a special file so I know what to do and not do around you."

"Then you must use the words correctly," Aine said. "*Beane sidhe*. What you're saying now is hardly appropriate."

Sunshine tried to say what Aine had said, but they'd reached the basement floor of the building. She used the excuse to back out of her Gaelic language lesson.

They found a set of stairs to the right of the old boiler that heated the building in cold weather. As they walked around it, there were groaning and settling sounds from the huge structure around them. Elevators growled going up and down the shaft and water gushed crankily through old pipes.

Sunshine didn't try to explain and cautioned Aine not to speak. Caeford lived another floor down. It was always better to be quiet around a dragon if they didn't know you were coming for a visit. A surprised dragon was rarely a happy dragon.

The stairs were narrow and filthy. Very few people used them. The sub-basement was necessary to the strength of the building's foundation, but it wasn't well maintained. Sunshine had found that people didn't care about what they couldn't see.

And yet here was Caeford's lair, their destination, hundreds of feet below ground. He had lived here since long before the city, or the building, hidden away from mankind in a series of caves. He'd adjusted as time had passed, but he never left the area where he'd been born.

As usual he was aware of the intrusion into his life. "Hello, Miss Merryweather. And this is your new associate?" He sniffed Aine. "The *beane sidhe* you spoke of. How fascinating. A woman of the ancient fairy world here in Norfolk."

"We're here because of your 'little' problem." Sunshine wiped her hands on a moist towelette and handed one to Aine. "We went to see the man who watched you fly away. He was dead—murdered in exactly the same way as John."

Caeford's large, tough face frowned. "You mean the werewolf. That's unfortunate."

"And the scent on the crime scene was the same," she continued.

"You're not seriously here to accuse me of killing them. Not here in my den, of all places. No one would be that stupid."

Sunshine faced him without any sign of fear. "That's exactly why we're here. I knew you were sending us to clean up your mess but not to clean up a dead body for you."

He growled deep in the back of his throat and a single plume of smoke came from one nostril. "It has been more than a century since I partook of human flesh."

"Is that a threat?" Sunshine demanded.

"No. A fact. Why kill one if you aren't going to eat it?"

His large yellow teeth were exposed to the dim light.

"That is no excuse," Aine told him. "I hunted a few of your ancestors who killed for sport."

He roared his anger, the sound bouncing back off the concrete walls making the noise ear splitting. "You dare tell me you hunted my kind?"

"Yes." She smiled. "And they were tasty too."

Sunshine put her hand on Aine's shoulder. "We're not here to get into a war about who hunted whose ancestors, Caeford. We want the truth about what happened to these men."

He backed down from his aggressive stance with Aine. "I did not kill the werewolf or the man on the roof. I knew you would handle the potential problem for me, Miss Merryweather. There was no reason to exert myself. This has been the basis of our relationship."

"Good. You won't mind if my *beane sidhe* gives you a sniff then?"

His yellow eyes widened in fury. "I see. Of course. Her people were very great hunters in the past—feared and tenacious. They made the werewolf look incompetent." He lowered his head to their level. "Please. Give me a good sniff, *beane sidhe*."

Sunshine hoped that he didn't take Aine's head off as he moved closer to her. She wasn't sure she would have been willing to take on the task, but Aine didn't seem to mind. She moved in close to Caeford, never losing eye contact with him. Their bodies were nearly touching.

Aine took a deep whiff of the dragon man. His scent was mixed with chemicals and herbs that she didn't recognize. But underlying it all was the deep, wild smell of dragon. It was completely different from the smell at the crime scenes.

"It's not him," she announced without as much as a tremor in her tone. She didn't move away from him, instead staring into his terrifying eyes. "Someone else is responsible for the deaths."

Caeford didn't move either. "I could snap you in half."

She smiled at him, nothing left of the middle-aged woman in the black cape. The crone with little flesh on her face and body, skeletal hands at her side, stood tall. "You'd find me a tough bit of bone to chew, dragon man."

He growled but took a step away from her. Sunshine hadn't realized until that moment that she was holding her breath, while her hands and thoughts were prepared for a spell to protect Aine if necessary.

Aine took a step back too, resuming her mostly human form in the black hood.

"We're leaving now." Sunshine tried not to sound as relieved as she felt. "As soon as I have more information, I'll let you know."

"Let me know if you need assistance in your quest as well," Caeford offered. "I don't want my name and reputation sullied over this mix up."

"As if anyone without magic would believe a dragon had killed these men," Sunshine said. "Do you have any idea what might have happened to them?"

"I do not," he said. "It seems to me that the first murder may have been deliberate and the second only used to throw off the scent of the trail. I'm sure the killer never dreamed of facing a *beane sidhe*. I have never been particularly interested in a human death. They are all the same to me. Learn what someone gained by killing John Lancaster, the first to die, and you may have all the answers you need. He was a good man-wolf. I should hate to see him go unavenged."

Sunshine started to thank him when there was a sound above them. Someone else was coming down the stairs into the dragon's lair.

He growled deep in the back of his throat and a single plume of smoke came from one nostril.

Chapter Eight

"It is O'Neill," Aine told her. "He and his partner may have followed us here thinking that we would lead them to the truth."

Sunshine didn't ask how she knew who it was before she could see—no doubt the scent of the pair. Bending her head, she began the threads of a magic defense shield that would hide the dragon from the two detectives and four uniformed officers who accompanied them.

"You do not need to hide me, witch," Caeford roared. "Let them come. I shall slay them all."

The old concrete pylons shook around them. Dust fell on their heads from the floor above.

"And that's exactly why you need to be hidden," Sunshine returned as calmly as if she were giving him a brownie recipe. "It's part of Purple Door Service. We protect our clients from those who wish them harm, as well as from their own shortsightedness. Be still and let them go, Caeford. Let's not make this a dragon hunt. We all know how that ends."

The dragon man was grudgingly silent with only a few smoky breaths that could have given him away. As the police officers entered the sub-basement with guns drawn, there was nothing but a large, empty, concrete cavern. When no real threat was perceived, the officers holstered their weapons as Malto sent them to search the edges of the shadowed perimeter.

O'Neill and Malto stared at the two women they had nearly followed to their deaths.

"Detective O'Neill," Sunshine greeted him. "Detective Malto. What a surprise. What brings you down here?"

"We could ask you the same thing." O'Neill stared at Aine. "You two are never far apart, are you?"

"We work together," Sunshine said. "I could say the same thing about you and your partner."

"What's going on down here?" Detective Malto demanded. "What are you two hiding?"

"Hiding?" Sunshine glanced around them. "We're not hiding anything. We were looking for the long-term parking lot. I've been thinking about moving the agency into this building. But the short-term parking is awful. Parking on the street would get to be old after a while. I like the building, but I just can't see it, can you, Aine?"

"I don't see anything." It was the safest answer she could think of since she had no idea what the witch was saying. Anything else could give them away by her ignorance of present-day situations.

"You're not as dimwitted as you'd like us to think," O'Neill challenged Aine.

"I'm sure that is true of you as well."

"I think she just called us stupid," Malto said. "Isn't there is a law about badmouthing police detectives?"

"We seem to simply be in the wrong place at the wrong

time." Sunshine intervened with a dazzling smile. "I'm sorry you came all the way down here for nothing, detectives. Next time, give me a call, and I'll tell you what we're doing. Come on, Aine. Let's get out of here."

With nothing to hold them, the police officers and detectives stepped out of their way to allow Aine and Sunshine to ascend the stairs to the next floor.

"What do you think they were really doing down here?" Malto thoughtfully asked her partner.

"I'm not sure I want to know." He shook his head after taking a look around. "Let's follow them. There's something they aren't telling us."

"You're telling me!"

When they'd reached the basement floor, Sunshine used a spell to get herself and Aine out of the building. She was tired of being followed by the police, and there was no harm in getting them out more quickly.

They found themselves on the street next to the purple convertible. It would be a long walk up the stairs to the building's main floor for the officers, O'Neill, and Malto. Sunshine had temporarily disabled the elevator to slow them down.

"Your magic is quite dizzying," Aine said as she got in the car. "Different than mine. I know the feel of it now, so I will recognize it in the future."

Sunshine wasn't sure if that was a warning or simply an observation. She didn't pause to think of it there. Instead she started the car and left Caeford's lair as quickly as evening traffic would allow.

"I knew Caeford wasn't stupid enough to do something like that," she said to Aine. "He would've taken care of it himself if he had. But that leaves us still guessing why John, and Harley Matthews were murdered."

"Perhaps the dragon man has given us a good suggestion," Aine said. "If Harley Matthews's murder was just a smokescreen for John Lancaster's death—to lead us in the wrong direction—that could be the only thing the two have in common. Any other inquiry into that line of thinking may lead us nowhere."

Sunshine hit the purple steering wheel with the palm of her hand in a fit of frustrated temper. "What would someone hope to gain by hiding John's death from me?"

"You mean besides their life? Whoever killed John would know that you would swear blood vengeance."

"I suppose that's true. I've never been tempted to kill another living soul—until now."

"Then we shall need to find the killer to ask that question, but taking the dragon man off our list, who does that leave behind?"

"It's not easy to kill a werewolf." Sunshine ran her hand through her hair. "I don't know what creature could have done it but it had to be strong and there had to be magic."

"We agree on that. I am unfamiliar with the creatures that dwell here. But surely none have enough magic that they would not fear your reprisal."

"Hey!" Sunshine smiled at her. "Thanks."

"It was not a compliment, merely an observation."

"I see. Well, thanks anyway. I'm kind of powerful. I keep it hidden so no one suspects. I don't want people to fear me, but it's nice to be respected."

Aine agreed. "You are moderately strong. But you certainly have potential."

Sunshine began going through a list of creatures that could have killed John and were present in the city. "Of course, another werewolf could fit the bill. Definitely Caeford, but he's one of a kind. I don't know of another dragon for thousands of miles, although I've heard of one in California. A really strong witch could have killed him, but I think we both would've sensed that much magic. And I don't see a witch making a mess like that, do you? There are a few older vampires around but they're kind of settled, you know?"

"Tame," Aine added. "What about local demons? Or other shapeshifters—besides one of your mouse woman's strength. Quite obviously, she could not have killed a wolf."

"There are other shifters." Sunshine shrugged. "I've met some of them. They could be powerful enough to kill John. I'll have Jane print a list of them for us to track down."

They made a quick stop at a small grocery store to resupply the office. When they finally got back to the agency, Jane was waiting anxiously at the door.

"I found something interesting about the man on the roof." Her eyes were glued on the bags in Sunshine's arms. "Did you get everything? I'm starving."

"Yes. I got everything. Show me what you found and you can eat." Sunshine held the bags away from Jane's twitching nose and eager hands.

"Oh. Of course. Let's look at the computer."

They gathered around the flat-screen monitor. Aine touched a finger to it and watched the screen's negative response. Sunshine laughed and told her that she should just look at it.

"I did a thorough search." Jane pulled up several dozen files. "Harley Matthews had some interesting clients at *Tattoo Hell*, including John."

"John had a tattoo done there?" Sunshine read quickly through the names on the receipts. "I see quite a few names that I recognize. Amos Johnson is a shifter—some kind of cat."

Jane yelped and started trembling.

"Don't worry," Sunshine told her. "I'm sure he's not looking for you."

"Thanks." Jane squeaked.

"What of the others?" Aine asked.

"Marcus Fletcher is another werewolf." Sunshine pointed out. "Tom Knox is a shifter. So is Irene Godfrey. It's like *Tattoo Hell* is making itself the go-to place for creatures in the area. But why kill John, and who killed Harley?"

Aine glanced at her. "What is the likelihood that this tattoo man was an innocent as he watched Caeford unfurl his wings? Perhaps he was there to challenge the dragon."

"Surely no human would be stupid enough to challenge a dragon," Sunshine said thoughtfully.

"I would have said the same about a human challenging a wolf," Aine added. "In my day, when men hunted a wolf, they went in a large pack, many times with witches who aided them in securing the wolf's death."

"Maybe Harley Matthews wanted to get Caeford as a client," Jane suggested in a timid voice.

"No matter what, it sounds like we need to pay a visit to *Tattoo Hell*." Sunshine looked at Aine. "How do you feel about getting a tattoo?"

Jane snatched the food bags from the desk and hurried with them into the kitchen area. Sunshine went to change clothes for something more appropriate and left Aine sitting at the computer.

It was a curious device that the *beane sidhe* carefully inspected. It didn't respond to any of her spoken magic. There was a long, black rope coming from it, possibly made of leather. It appeared to be the tail of the beast. She pulled the end of it from a hole in the wall. The colorful, lighted box went dark.

"What did you do?" Jane skittered from the kitchen. "It took me a long time to get that information together. Lucky for you I made copies of everything. You shouldn't touch things when you don't understand them."

Normally Aine's response to the young woman wouldn't have been pleasant. She wasn't one to ignore a challenge. Part of her reluctance to do anything but nod to the creature was her background. The other part was expecting something in return.

"Show me. I am very interested in this magic."

Jane sat down with a careful laugh. "It's not magic. It's science. This is a computer. You pulled the plug from the wall where it gets the power. When it stays plugged in, electricity passes from the wall into the machine. This is how you start it."

Aine watched her movements carefully. As long as O'Neill lived in this place, she would be bound here with him, in one form or another. It was good to learn the things of this time.

"Thank you, Jane. Now show me information on O'Neill as you showed Sunshine about Harley Matthews."

"Okay. I can do that. He'll be easier since he works for the police department." Jane had to wait for the computer to finish rebooting and then typed Sean Patrick O'Neill into the search bar.

Instantly there were hundreds of men with the same name. Jane weeded through them, adding search criteria until she found the man they were looking for. In another moment, everything about O'Neill was on the screen—from his job as a police detective to his home address, the gym where he worked out, the bank he frequented, even the finance company that held the loan on his car.

"See?" Jane smiled brightly at Aine. "And this is only the beginning. If I wanted to, I could tell you what he had for breakfast this morning."

"What about a lover?"

"You don't think it's the other detective, Malto, do you?"

"No. There is no sign of affection between them. There must be another—perhaps the raven-haired woman at the…"

"Pizzeria," Jane finished for her. "It might take a few minutes, but I can probably find something if there's a serious woman in his life."

Aine stood up straight. "Of course there is a woman in his life. The O'Neills have always been susceptible to the female influence."

"Okay. I'll be glad to help."

Sunshine was back as they finished speaking. She

noticed how pleased Jane looked, even though she wasn't eating. It was unusual for her. She normally had two modes—hunger and fear.

"What did you say to Jane?" she asked Aine as they were leaving for *Tattoo Hell.*

"I asked for her help with the magic box to locate O'Neill's current lover."

"You don't think it's Malto? They seemed pretty tight— except for the honey at the pizzeria. Is that who you're thinking of?"

"I don't know." Aine inspected Sunshine's change of clothing. "Is this what is considered necessary for the tattoo shop?"

Sunshine looked down at her jeans and tank top beneath a gray trench coat. "This is trendier than what I was wearing. You should fit right in. You look kind of Goth, or whatever they're calling it now."

"But I do not require a drawing…tattoo…on my person. In my day, a witch could be burned for such a thing."

"Don't worry. Not much witch burning going on right now. You can hold my hand so I don't scream when I get my tattoo."

Aine looked at her sharply. "Is that what you require?"

"Maybe. We have to blend in if we expect to get good info." Sunshine opened the car. "This should be quite an experience."

Chapter Nine

Sunshine followed the GPS unerringly to the tattoo shop on the other side of town. Of course Norfolk, being a Navy town, had a history of tattoos and tattoo artists. *Tattoo Hell* was a newer store set in a bevy of psychic readers and nail shops, but it stood out with its flaming sign and giant devil's head coming out of the middle.

The shop wasn't busy. Only two artists were there with a few friends hanging around comparing their recent tattoos. Everyone noticed when the women walked in.

A younger man came to greet them. "I'm Michel." He grinned. "Like Michelangelo?" He laughed at his own joke as he sized up Sunshine from her high-heeled, black boots to the top of her frizzy hair. "What can I do to you?"

Sunshine giggled and put on a sweet, stupid smile. "You know, we were just daring each other to get some ink tonight. I was thinking of a simple pentagram on my arm. What do you think?"

"Sounds fun to me, pretty lady. Step into my parlor." He indicted a lounge chair behind him. "What about your girlfriend?"

"I do not require your services, boy," Aine told him. "But I will remain at her side."

"Okay. Let's draw a few pentagrams and see what gets you going. What's your name?"

"Sunshine Merryweather." She put her hand in his to have him help her into the lounge.

"Awesome name." One of the other young men wandered their way to watch the procedure. "Your parents must've been hippies. Or is that a stage name?"

"Nope," she responded. "It's all mine."

Michel drew some pentacles. Some were plain while others had flourishes and embellishments on them. "You can start with something simple and add on later."

"Sounds good. Let's do the basic." Sunshine almost backed out of it when she saw the tattoo needles and ink. "Maybe even half a pentagram would be good."

"The Celts had tattoos, though they didn't refer to them as such," Aine said. "They were mostly done with woad and sharp objects used to puncture the skin. Many of them proved to be fatal through infection. But they were tribal people who lost great numbers during battle and didn't seem to mind dying for other causes as well."

When she'd stopped speaking, everyone was staring at her. Sunshine laughed to break the tension brought on by the hypnotic monotone of the *beane sidhe*.

"Sure. Okay." Michel shook his head to clear it. "We'll do the basic pattern."

The other two people in the shop stood close to watch. Sunshine closed her eyes and invoked a spell to help her relax and another to make sure the tattoo was safe and painless.

As Michel focused on what he was doing, she asked about other tattoos he'd done.

"I do hundreds a week. Some are really elaborate. Some are simple like yours."

"I have a friend who had his ink done here," she continued. "Maybe you remember him, John Lancaster."

"Really?" One of the watchers was immediately interested. "I know that name from somewhere."

"My friend," Sunshine continued. "Do you know him, Michel?"

"Yeah. I remember him. Big man. Dark hair." He didn't look up from her arm. The drone of the tattoo gun hummed.

"He was killed this week. They found him dead in an alley by the mall." Sunshine watched his face closely. "Did you hear about it?"

"No. I didn't hear that. I'm sorry. He seemed like a good guy."

Aine discerned a slight variation in his tone and a small twitch to his mouth. "Did you know John outside this establishment?"

"I only met him once. He was Harley's customer." Michel's gaze wandered for an instant. "Are you cops or something?"

"We're not cops," Sunshine assured him. "But we did hear that something bad happened to Harley today. I'll bet you know about that too."

"Look, I have to concentrate to get this right. I can't talk at the same time."

"I understand." Sunshine knew they were getting to him. "We can always talk when you're done."

Michel looked even more nervous at that idea. His hand shook a little, but the spell kept the pentagram straight. The other tattoo artist urged the remaining customers out the front door and slowly put up the closed sign.

Aine watched his furtive movements as he moved away from the door to a cabinet at the side of the room. She could hear his heart beating fast—too fast for his slow movements. He was trying to throw them off and was planning an attack.

She stood to her full height, the hag taking over her appearance as she raised a skeletal arm and pointed at him. "Stop," she commanded. "You shall not move."

The artist stopped in full stride, eyes glazed, mouth hanging open. There was a small caliber handgun in his grasp.

"I didn't know you could do that," Sunshine said to her. "There's definitely more to you than just a pretty face."

"Pretty face?" Michel stared at Aine in horror. "Who are you two? What do you want?"

Sunshine sat up on the lounge and examined the finished pentagram on her plump arm. "Not bad. I might want to come back for a few of those flourishes. But for now, I want to know what you and your friends have been up to."

He shook his head. "Nothing. We haven't done anything. You have the wrong place."

"You don't know anything about your clientele being werewolves, shifters, that kind of thing? Is that what you want me to believe?"

"What?" He stared at both women, but quickly averted his gaze from Aine's horrific countenance. "There's no such thing, right? I mean, those things don't exist."

"You tell me." Sunshine put a carefully manicured purple fingernail under his chin. "Do you think they exist?"

Her magic swirled around him. Aine could see it, and saw the change that came over him.

"Okay. We get a lot of talkers in here. People get comfortable, and they want to tell you their whole life story. A few of them told us some wild tales. Then Harley was approached by some chick who offered him money if he'd help her do a few things."

"What kind of things?" Sunshine asked.

"It sounds goofy, but she gave us names and asked us to stick them and collect some of their blood. It wasn't much—just a dot on a napkin. She was willing to pay a lot of money. What difference did it make? It didn't hurt them or anything."

"What difference indeed," Aine growled.

"Blood magic." Sunshine nodded. "If you were doing what this woman asked of you, why is Harley dead?"

"I don't know. I swear I don't know. John was the first one that we took a drop of blood from. We didn't think it had anything to do with his death. I mean, how could it?"

"Who is this woman that hired you?" Aine asked.

Michel laughed nervously. "Harley was the only one who made contact with her. I don't know who she is or where she comes from. That's the truth. We were scared when we heard he was killed. We figure that chick was bad news. She might've even killed him. She might come after us too."

"That's all I can think of." Sunshine glanced at Aine. "You?"

"They may have the names of their next victims," Aine replied. "Perhaps a list that Jane can look up on the magic box."

"Good idea." Sunshine grinned. "Mr. Bad was so right about you. Michel, give us that list."

He moved away from the fingernail that had held him in place and scrounged around in a drawer until he found a list of five names. Only John's name had been crossed off.

Aine sniffed the list. "Written in human blood."

"Okay, Michel and—" she glanced sharply at the second tattoo artist still frozen under Aine's spell—"what's your name?"

Aine nodded and freed him.

"Ike." His voice broke like a teenager's.

"Michel. Ike." Sunshine gazed at them with unforgettable blue eyes. "All of this is going to seem like a dream to you after we're gone. Forget the list. Forget the mystery chick. Forget John.   None of this ever happened. Mourn your friend. Keep doing these awesome tattoos. Don't be so greedy."

Both men blinked as they watched two women walk out of *Tattoo Hell.*

"I need a drink." Michel ran his hand around the back of his neck. "That last one took a lot out of me."

"I think it looked great though, man," Ike said. "I could use an early night."

* * *

"Human blood," Aine said when they were in the convertible and headed back to the agency. "We must be mistaken about the magic. It has to be a witch tearing people to shreds. I know of no other creature that would use blood in this manner."

"No way. There's no way a witch did this. I would've sensed it. I would've felt the magic."

"I think your bond with the wolf clouds your judgment."

Sunshine glared at her. "I don't care what you think. I'm not blinded by my love for John. And if that were the case, why couldn't you sense the magic at the crime scenes? I'm telling you this is something else that uses blood magic."

"Perhaps you're correct." Aine understood her partner's agitation over the death of her lover. "I do not know of any other creature that uses blood to hunt for their victims and destroy them in such a manner, but that doesn't mean there isn't one."

"Werewolves sometimes use blood to hunt for their victims," Sunshine agreed. "But I can't imagine one of them planning something this way. Usually if they want to kill you, they kill you. But since this is like nothing I've seen before, I could be wrong about that too."

"Is there a pack? Could this be a pack dispute for leadership?"

"I don't know. I can ask around. But John wasn't the pack leader and had no interest in taking that position. He usually didn't stay in one place that long. He was a loner."

"It could be possible that the pack leader misjudged John. A few carefully placed questions could bear fruit. I would be happy to undertake this for you. I know your heart is not in it."

Sunshine pulled the convertible into the agency parking lot. "My heart might be broken by John's death, but the rest of me is ready for revenge. You don't have to worry about my commitment."

"I shall await word from you on that inquiry then." Aine inclined her head.

"Thanks." Sunshine grabbed her bag. "You really had my back in there. I appreciate it. You're going to make a wonderful partner. Will you contact O'Neill tonight?"

"Yes. The time is right for him to know me—and himself."

"Well, let me know how that goes. Maybe once he knows you and himself he'll get off our tails with his homicide investigation."

    * * *

After spending hundreds of years as the *beane sidhe* for the O'Neill family, Aine was nervous as she prepared herself for that night. It was absurd, almost beyond belief, that her hands would tremble as she thought of the task ahead of her. How many O'Neills had she gone to this way? It was true that most of them were adolescent, but it should make no difference.

She stared at the crescent moon in the black sky above her. It was possibly the only thing older than her in this city. "How many times have you stared down at me?" she asked the glowing white circle. "How many dreams did you take from me?"

It was also unusual for her not to be in the same dwelling with the O'Neill she haunted. She'd been with the family for so long it was getting difficult to remember when she didn't serve them. It was no great hardship for her to go to his home—Aine was not a creature of flesh and blood unless she chose to be. The woman who would enter Sean O'Neill's dreams would be the ghost of her former self.

Because it was customary, Aine stood outside O'Neill's home and moaned in her most piteous voice. She stared at the second story window where his 'apartment'—Sunshine's words—was located. She reached for him with long gaunt arms and wept for his ultimate death. It was the way of the *beane sidhe* to begin the long process.

No one ventured close to their windows that night to discover where the terrifying sound came from. Some in the building turned on their lights and shivered beneath their blankets, praying for morning.

When the preliminary announcement was made, Aine allowed herself to drift into O'Neill's bedroom.

He was alone in his room. He'd been asleep for a few hours. A smaller version of Jane's magic box was open on the bed beside him with a picture of the Purple Door Detective Agency on the screen.

There were other accoutrements of his life and profession. He slept with a gun under his pillow. His gray suit was carelessly tossed on a chair. There were pictures of his parents on a nearby dressing table—no photos of a sister or brother. He was the last of his family line.

Aine watched him sleep for a moment, realizing the profound change his life would take when he realized he was not alone and would never be alone again in his lifetime. The secrets she would impart to him were for him alone and could never be shared with another. That was the sacred vow between them.

"Ach! I am happy beyond words to be here at your side, O'Neill. Prepare yourself. I am coming for you."

O'Neill sat up in bed, gun in hand, and faced her. "What the hell are you doing here?"

Chapter Ten

Such a thing had never happened to Aine in all her long years of haunting the O'Neill family. She gaped like the goldfish in the bowl for a moment before she found her voice.

"Go back to sleep," she hissed. "You cannot be awake at this moment. Sleep, O'Neill."

As *beane sidhe* magic went, it was poorly done, but her excuse—to find him awake and staring at her—was enough. What should she do if he didn't fall unconscious?

"I think I need to be awake right now. What's your name—Ann?" The gun stayed steady on her face as did his suspicious and angry gaze.

"I am Aine of Ulster," she corrected. "And you cannot be awake. The first time must be in a dream. I cannot come to you with glad tidings while you are awake."

"Glad tidings?" He got to his feet slowly, glancing around the room as he turned on the bedside lamp. "Is it

Christmas already? You don't look like an angel. Let's try
again. What are you doing here?"

Aine was nearly beside herself trying to decide how to
correct the situation. She had never faced another like it. It
was possible that she would have to give up this poor attempt
at communication and leave him. She must have been more
affected by coming to this foreign place than she realized.

"I apologize, O'Neill." She slightly inclined her head. "I
shall return at another time."

"Stay where you are," he commanded. "I'm calling for
backup. I knew you had something to do with those murders.
You and Little Miss Sunshine. Did you really think you
could rip me apart too? Was I getting too close to the truth
for you?"

"No." Instead of guilt and remorse, anger suddenly came
to her at his ignorance. "I am not here to harm you, fool. I am
here to offer you a great gift—a gift you have never seen the
like of before. You are the last of your bloodline to receive
this gift."

Alarm changed the focus of his attention. "Did you
already kill Malto?"

"I have killed no one as of late, though I am sorely
tempted to snap your neck at this moment. Surely the O'Neill
bloodline has thinned and grown cold to have produced the
likes of you. Perhaps in your last dying moments you would
comprehend. I have never known even an O'Neill to be as
stubborn."

He'd picked up his cell phone as she spoke and punched
in his partner's number. "Malto? Are you okay?"

"Who is this? O'Neill? Have you got a mental problem?
It's two a.m. Go back to bed."

When his partner had abruptly ended her side of the
conversation, O'Neill stared at Aine again. "You're lucky
she's still safe."

"I have no reason to harm her."

"I'm calling the station."

As he began to use the phone again, Aine waved her hand, and the phone died. He hit it against the edge of the night stand a few times, but nothing happened.

"That's okay. Sit down in that chair." He waved the gun toward the chair with his suit on it. He grabbed two ties and prepared to strap her to the seat.

She laughed, turning from the middle-aged form in black to the hideous crone. "You will not bind me, O'Neill. Sit down. Put that weapon on the table."

Her ghastly voice and commanding form brought compliance. He tried to look away from her after he was seated, but she had compelled him to face her. "What do you want from me? How can you change the way you look? Did you inject me with drugs while I was sleeping? That's a felony, you know. You could spend the rest of your life in prison."

Aine stayed where she was. It was difficult to control her temper but necessary. Only in calm could she relate to the most important man in her life. She began to comb her long gray hair through her fingers as she spoke in a sing-song voice.

"Your family has existed for many years with different branches of the O'Neill bloodline. Hundreds of years ago, a Queen of Ulster took to her breast a false lover who accused your family of terrible crimes."

As she spoke, her countenance changed to the young, beautiful queen in the green velvet dress. Her fiery hair spilled down her back and across her shoulders. She wore a gold crown regally on her head. The emeralds in her ears and around her throat matched the color of her eyes.

"The queen believed her lover who had told her that he was wronged by the O'Neill family. She led the group that went to O'Neill castle and killed a great many of your family. In doing this, she doomed herself to haunt the O'Neills after she had passed through the underworld. She exists only as a *beane sidhe* to serve the family. For hundreds of years after she passed, she was friend, advisor, and protector to your ancestors."

Hazy images of the O'Neill family through generations in Ireland passed before O'Neill's amazed eyes, holding him in thrall. He saw his long-dead family members during the stages of their lives with a shadowy figure that greeted them at birth, came to them in adolescence to tell them their story, and held their hands at the moment of death to guide them to the underworld.

"I am Aine, Queen of Ulster, descendent of the *Fae* and the *Tuatha de Danaan*. I confess to you my sin against your family, which brings me to serve you, as is traditional. I regret I could not be here for several generations, including the start of your own life. I was held against my will at Castle O'Neill and only woke there recently. I immediately came to find you and relate your story. I am in your service from now until the day you die. I shall announce your death three times before it comes to you. I swear to you my fealty and that I shall be next to you as you travel to the underworld."

Aine changed to the middle-aged woman in the black cloak and then to the ragged crone as she continued to comb through her waist-length hair.

When she had stopped telling the story, the spell on O'Neill was lifted. He stared at her without speaking for several moments.

"Are you here to announce my death for the first time?" he asked.

"No. I should have come to you as a young man in a dream and told you what the bond between us is. Because I was spelled to a two-hundred-year sleep, this was not possible. Thus I am here now and will serve you and your descendants."

"You can't die because of the wrong you did my family hundreds of years ago. Is that right?"

She nodded. Her eyeless face was before him like a nightmare he couldn't awaken from.

"I release you. I think you've gained absolution. Is that possible for me to do?"

"No. Other O'Neills have tried. I am here until I am no longer. When the moment of my freedom is at hand, I shall be gone." She didn't tell him that the moment might come at the time of his death if he didn't have children of his own. It was not her place to give him that information.

"I knew the first time I saw you at the pizzeria. I recognized you even though you had changed so much compared to the painting."

"Painting?"

"My father died when I was a baby. I never knew anyone from the O'Neill side of the family. My mother raised me, but she kept a few things that he wanted passed down to me. One of them is an antique miniature. Wait. Let me show you."

He moved experimentally, like a man who wasn't sure if he was still under his own control. Aine stayed where she was and watched him. He was only partially clad in thin shorts, leaving his lean, muscular body open to her perusal.

Something moved inside her. It hadn't moved for centuries. She'd thought it as dead as the rest of her.

O'Neill impatiently pulled out a small wood chest and rummaged through it with a careless hand until he came to a tiny, oval-shaped portrait. "My mother thought this must be an ancestor of mine. She said my father told her that it had been passed down in my family for a couple hundred years. You see? It's you."

Aine peered at it as he stood close holding the likeness. It was a portrait that she had never sat for and yet it was her in her younger form. She touched it with a careful finger.

"It is quite remarkable. He must have painted it from memory." She glanced at the current O'Neill. "Jamie O'Neill was a talented painter, but because of family obligations, his paintings were limited to his life at the castle. He never told me about this. He must have painted it years before I led him to the underworld."

"Wow. My family had a castle?"

She slowly smiled at his childlike inquiry. "Yes. Castle O'Neill still stands. It is in ruins but still there."

"I'll have to go see it sometime." He ran his hand through his thick brown hair. "I have a thousand questions I'd like to ask you. This is amazing!"

"Amazing?"

"Yes. I have a *beane sidhe*. How cool is that? You have magic, right? Turn back into that pretty form again. How do you do that? Can you teach me to do it?"

Aine raised her hand. "Sleep, O'Neill. You have learned enough for one night."

He collapsed, snoring, on the rug at her feet.

She took the portrait with her. Perhaps he didn't mean her to have it. If so, she would return it. But it was pleasant to look upon as she had once looked upon herself in still water and polished surfaces. It reminded her of who she had been. Possibly not a good thing, but one she wanted to indulge for a brief time.

With her proper introduction to O'Neill over, Aine went back to the room in the brick building with the purple doors. She hadn't had a room of her own since her death. She wasn't sure what to do with it since she didn't sleep and kept no personal possessions. Now she put the small portrait on a side table near the window and stared out at the night that enfolded the city.

She finally left the room and soundlessly wandered the halls of the brick building. The mouse and the witch slept and dreamed on the same floor. There was little furniture in the two floors above. No one had lived here in some time. Ghosts moved like winding sheets through the dusty space, wondering why they lingered.

Aine glided through the darkness, thinking about the past and knowing she would have to return to Castle O'Neill if she ever wanted to discover who had spelled her into missing the last dozen or so family members she should have served. Not being there for those nameless O'Neills might mean she would not find release when Sean O'Neill passed from the world.

What then? Even she, who had seen the underworld and tasted death, shuddered and wept to think what was left for her.

Aine no longer had a heart or any other living organ in her dried body, but anger and the thirst for revenge—the same qualities that had doomed her as Queen of Ulster—began to rage. But it was different than when she was alive. Now she could observe the storm within her without being part of it.

An almost imperceptible force called to her through the dark passages and empty rooms. She surrendered to its summons and found herself in the downstairs office that belonged to Mr. Bad.

"I assume you found your O'Neill." His voice was soft yet commanding. Nuances of power hid in it.

"Yes. It was an unusual experience."

"Not surprising." His chair squeaked as he moved in it. "Tell me, Aine, what do you make of these deaths that you and Miss Merryweather are looking into?"

"Perhaps it is old magic—the kind that no longer exists."

He chuckled. "Many would say such about you."

"And you."

"Yes."

"I would say they are wrong. What do you make of the deaths?"

"I believe it is more than magic, Aine. I believe a creature from the furthest depths of the past may be responsible. I am not certain if Miss Merryweather can fight such a creature."

"You lack faith in the witch, sir?"

"Not faith. She has a good heart, and her magic is strong. But this creature cannot be destroyed by ordinary magic or ordinary weapons."

Aine considered the legions of creatures from werewolves to pookas that she had seen in her lifetime. "Are you saying the creature cannot be defeated?"

"I am saying that I suspect slaying this creature might take more than physical skill and magic. When the time is right, there must be a union of the two—including modern weaponry. Even then I have my doubts as to the outcome."

"Who are you?" Aine didn't hesitate to ask the question Sunshine would never have asked.

"Who do you think I am?"

"I have felt power such as yours only once in my existence. I do not like to put a name to it, and yet all the signs are there. I ask myself, why would he be here among the living?"

He laughed, rich and hearty enough to shake the office. "Put your suspicions aside, Aine of Ulster. No doubt you know my name. Others of this time do not. I would rather you didn't help them remember. I am here for a purpose which I can't name, but it is not to hurt those around me. Can you do that?"

She nodded. "I can indeed, my lord. Others will not hear your true name from my lips."

"Thank you. I bid you goodnight then."

Chapter Eleven

Sunshine awakened as she always did—with a new perspective on life—eager to decide what she would wear that day.

She brushed her temperamental hair and washed her face with a special herbal mixture that she'd created for herself. She looked into her clear, blue eyes and smiled at her beautiful face in the mirror.

"I know things went badly yesterday," she told her reflection. "But things will be better today."

Her reflection didn't agree with her. "What's going to make it better? John is still dead. Or have you forgotten already? You have limited information as to who killed him. Where are you going from here?"

She hated it when her reflection was negative. "There are several possibilities now. I can feel the threads being pulled together."

"But are you at the heart of that? Or is it just an

illusion?"

"I don't have time for this today. You need to go back to sleep and wake up on the right side of the bed."

"Which side is that?" her reflection yelled back at her as she left the bathroom. "Wait a minute. We have more to discuss."

"Not right now. I'll see you later."

Choosing a bright yellow dress that went well with her hair, Sunshine added purple jewelry and wore purple sandals that tied on her ankles. Everything went with purple. She avoided looking at herself in the mirror again. She needed to be on her toes if she was going to be able to use the information they had uncovered from the tattoo shop.

Aine and Jane were already in the office by the time Sunshine arrived downstairs. It surprised her how well the pair of opposites seemed to get along after Jane's initial fear. Usually it took her longer to trust someone. Her mind was still caught up in a small rodent's thought processes even though she could take on the size and shape of a woman.

"Good morning, ladies." Sunshine went into the kitchen to get a cup of tea. "What are we looking at?"

"I looked up everything I could find about Detective O'Neill." Jane glanced at Sunshine. "That was per her request as a new associate."

"That's fine," Sunshine said. "You were right to accommodate her. What did you find?"

Jane smiled nervously. "I found everything you can possibly imagine about his life. It's like he doesn't do anything he's worried about hiding. Everything was in plain view—including his girlfriend."

Sunshine and Aine stared at the screen as the beautiful, lush, black-haired woman from the pizzeria smiled back at them. She had brilliant blue eyes and a wide mouth that was made for passion.

"Who is she?" Aine inquired. "Can you find an image of her that shows the rest of her body? She seems thin to me. A woman needs large hips to carry healthy children."

"Her name is Elena Spiros. This is her picture from her driver's license," Jane explained. "It only shows faces, I'm afraid."

"What does she do?" Sunshine asked with a glance at Aine. "Believe me, these days you can tell more about someone who plans to have children by the job they do."

"She's an artist." Jane brought up a group of pictures displaying Elena's work. "Her paintings are wonderful, very expressive."

The three women studied the colorful paintings as the computer scrolled through them.

"An artist." Sunshine shrugged. "You have a much better chance of O'Neill having children with an artist than say a stockbroker or his police partner."

"Good." Aine smiled in a satisfied manner. "The search was well done. Thank you, Jane."

"What about seeing him last night?" Sunshine blew on her hot herb tea before she sipped it. "Did you visit him? Are things straight between you now?"

The front door to the office opened abruptly bringing in the scent of sea air, the traffic sounds of the city, and O'Neill.

"I'm just wondering if it's okay if I tell my girlfriend about you." He grinned at Aine. "Good morning, Sunshine. Miss Smith."

"I guess that answers the question." Sunshine took Jane into the kitchen.

"I'm sorry." O'Neill watched them go. "Was it a secret? Do they know about you?"

"Most assuredly they do. But others should not be trusted with this knowledge," Aine told him. She'd never seen an O'Neill so exuberant about what she had told him. Most were humbled and sobered with the thought of their own mortality.

"Elena is completely trustworthy," he assured her. "We're not married yet, but we might be someday. If you're going to be in my life, she should know about you. Probably my partner should too. I mean, what if I'm shot and dying in an alley and you come along to grab me to take me to the underground? She wouldn't know what to think, and she might even shoot you."

Aine looked into his young face wondering if she had ever been as young. "Telling your wife is up to you. Telling your children is essential. Telling friends and men you sport with would be wrong. And it is the underworld, not underground."

His blue eyes clouded. "Sorry. I'm still new at this. Is there somewhere I can search for it? I got up this morning and checked Google. There were a lot of references to the *beane sidhe*, but I wasn't sure what was real and what wasn't."

Jane's head popped around the corner from the kitchen. "Google. He's talking about the magic box."

Sunshine yanked her back with an apology to her associate.

"I do not pretend to know everything about this time. I will be happy to tell you what you want to know about the *beane sidhe* and the underworld. I'm not sure what can be gained by checking your Google for information."

"That's okay." He reached out to squeeze her shoulder. "I didn't even think about you being new to this century. Let's set up another time to talk. I'm still working those homicides, but I might not be back too late. Do you have a cell phone yet?"

Aine gasped when he touched her. For only an instant, she was the young Queen of Ulster again, in the spring of her life, all the magic of living and love before her.

For all her contact with the O'Neill family in the past, she hadn't been touched by another person since her death. The earlier family knew the rules and boundaries. She would have to assume that her O'Neill was as clueless about how to be with her as she was about Google and a cell phone.

She rubbed her shoulder where he'd touched her. It felt odd, as though power had surged through her. She returned immediately to her form as the middle-aged woman in black. What had caused the change? It was disorienting for her even though she recovered quickly.

"I shall contact you," she promised, glad that he hadn't seen her change. "We have many things to discuss."

"Sounds good." He glanced toward the kitchen where Sunshine and Jane were spying on them. "And don't worry— I know all of you are innocent of those killings. I'm not sure yet what's going on, but Malto and I will find out."

He said goodbye and started to leave when a call came through on his cell phone. He walked to the side of the room as Sunshine and Jane came out of the kitchen.

When he turned back, he had a grim appearance. "You two were busy last night, weren't you?"

Sunshine was happy to respond. "We're always busy. What's up?"

"Have you ever heard of *Tattoo Hell*?" His gaze flashed to her and Aine. "Don't bother answering. The police already have the video footage of your visit. Malto took one look, and she's raging for arrest warrants for you."

"What are you talking about, O'Neill?" Sunshine demanded.

"I'm talking about the last two owners of *Tattoo Hell* being found dead at their shop this morning. Do I need to tell you that they were ripped to pieces just like John Lancaster and Harley Matthews?"

Sunshine's eyes narrowed before replying. "Excuse us a minute."

Aine followed her into her office.

"Did you do this?" Sunshine asked in a hoarse voice.

"No. I had no reason to kill those men. They were not a threat to O'Neill."

"Okay. Just checking." The witch leaned close to her. "What was that with the quick change when he touched you?

Is that supposed to happen because you haunt him?"

"Your questions annoy me." Aine walked by her and out into the main office.

"Sorry about that." Sunshine appeared right behind her. "That seems like a huge coincidence, I know. Believe me, they were healthy when we left them."

"But you don't have any idea what happened?" he asked her.

"Not right now," she said. "Aine? Any ideas?"

"No."

"Jane?" Sunshine asked.

"I get it. You don't know." O'Neill stopped her. "I'll keep my partner off your backs, but if you hear anything, let me know. I'll see you later, Aine."

When he was gone, Sunshine's hair poofed up like a lion's mane around her face. "Did you hear that? Michel and Ike are both dead now too. We have to figure this out before anyone else is killed."

"You did not tell him about the names we have or that we know blood from each of those men who got tattoos was taken by a chick," Aine mentioned.

Jane giggled. "Really? They were attacked by chicks?"

Sunshine sighed heavily. "All right—one of you learn the lingo. Otherwise I can't promise you'll be safe. A chick is slang for a woman. So we're looking for a woman who may be the killer or may be someone working with the killer. Are we clear on that?"

Aine and Jane nodded.

"Do you have those names?" Jane asked.

"Yes." Sunshine got them from her handbag. "I knew all of them. They used to hang around with John sometimes. They're all shifters. Why would someone want to kill a group of shifters?"

"What about Harley Matthews and the other two at *Tattoo Hell*?" Jane asked.

"I think we should start a magic board on all this,"

Sunshine said. "To the Bat Cave, ladies."

Neither woman had any idea what she was talking about. Sunshine told them to come into her office and gave up trying to explain.

Once in her office, Sunshine's magic pulled up a clear, flat space. She used her finger to write on it.

"We have Harley Matthews and his friends at *Tattoo Hell*, who were approached to give our suspect blood samples from a group of shifters and werewolves which included John."

Sunshine wrote their names on the board, and their faces appeared beside them. She only faltered a moment when she stared at John's image.

"Now. We have no name and no image for the chick." Sunshine created the image of a cute baby chicken with a question mark over it. "We know that Harley was killed because he asked for more money from the chick. We don't know why the other two were killed."

"The chick might be aware that they spoke with us last night," Aine said. "We have to assume that she has magic and may have spelled them to know if they spoke out of turn."

Jane wiped a tear from her eye. "You may have killed the other two without knowing it."

"We had no choice." Sunshine touched the spot where Michel had put the pentagram on her arm. Despite her healing spell, there was still some redness around the image. "If we're going to get to the bottom of this, we must all assume some risk."

The front door opened again. Jane dried her tears and went to see who was there.

"Good job with O'Neill," Sunshine commended Aine. "I don't think we'll have to worry about him and Malto again."

"Though I assume you understand that I did not give him the information for that purpose."

"Of course not." Sunshine stared at the magic board.

"What does the chick want with the shifters? Why kill them?"

"Assuming that she is the killer," Aine said. "I believe she has made it clear that she wants their deaths."

"Yes. But why? None of these men are the types to lead packs or wield influence. Why kill them?"

"Was there anything different or unusual about your lover before he died?"

Sunshine swallowed hard. "I don't think so. John and I had a strong bond, but I didn't see him every day. He didn't live here. It was a loose relationship. He needed his space, and I needed mine."

"So you did not observe him on the day of his death?" Aine asked.

"No. I hadn't seen him for a few days. He texted me the night before he was killed, but he didn't say anything about being in danger. I don't know what he was mixed up in."

"It is imperative that we speak with the other shifters on the list before they too are killed and we are left with no answers as to who wanted them dead."

"You're right." Sunshine said. "I don't have any of their phone numbers, so we'll have to track them down. I should have thought of it last night. I hope they aren't all dead already."

Chapter Twelve

Jane came back into Sunshine's office. "There's a potential client in the waiting room. Are we taking on new clients right now?"

"Of course," Sunshine said. "We have to pay the bills. I want to know what happened to John, but no one is paying us to check into it. Aine, take a seat and keep that middle-aged look going. Jane, show in our new client."

The potential new client was looking for a friend of his that had gone missing a few days before. Lloyd Samson said his friend was more responsible than to just disappear. "We play in a band together, and he missed last night's gig. We share a place and rent is due. I've known Amos all my life. He's just not this kind of dude."

Sunshine didn't have to look at her list to know this was one of the shifters. "We'll be happy to look for your friend, Lloyd. Jane, get him a missing person's document to fill out."

Lloyd thanked her. He was a good-looking young man, as most shifters tended to be. It seemed to be a trait of nature, possibly meant to keep shifters safe in society.

Jane got him a form to fill out and led him back out into the main office.

"Ye have to tell him what we suspect," Aine said. "He could be in danger like the others."

"I didn't see a tattoo, did you? And if we tell him, he might not be willing to help us."

"You plan to take his money to find someone we were looking for anyway?"

"I know you don't get the whole burden of finances, but I don't conjure up money," Sunshine explained. "The agency has to take on paying clients. That's how we pay our taxes, power, and other expenses."

Lloyd finished filling out his form and returned to her office. Jane stared hard at Sunshine, her hands nervously wringing the paper before she gave it to her.

Sunshine sighed. "All right. I get it. Lloyd, we have to tell you something. We knew Amos was missing already. He might be in danger. You might be in danger too. Do you have any tattoos from *Tattoo Hell*?"

He shook his tawny mane. "I wouldn't put anything like that on this body." He pulled off his t-shirt to reveal nothing but a broad expanse of tanned, muscled skin. "Tell me what you think happened to Amos. Maybe I can help."

"All right then." Sunshine had feasted her eyes on his body for long enough—besides, he was already putting on his shirt. "We found out last night that a group of shifters may be targeted." She explained the situation and told him about John's death.

"Wow. That's some really bad stuff." He frowned. "I know the other three shifters. I just saw Irene last night. Maybe I can help you out with them if you'll help me with Amos."

Sunshine glared at both her associates, who'd questioned

her judgment. "I think that would be appropriate, Lloyd. Thank you."

"I want to pay you anyway. John was a friend of mine. He was always going on about what a great place this was for people like us to get help. You need money to keep going, right?" He grinned and put a large handful of wadded-up bills on her desk.

"I appreciate your understanding." She gestured to Jane to take the money.

Aine and Sunshine asked Lloyd a few more questions about the last time he'd seen Amos and if the cat shifter had been in any trouble.

"Not as far as I know. He was looking forward to the gig he missed as much as I was. It's tough to get a new band started."

They exchanged phone numbers and agreed to meet that night at a club frequented by the shifter community. Lloyd said he'd ask around about other shifters with tattoos and call if he had any news.

"I'm so glad you came in today." Sunshine put her hand in his much larger one.

"Oh hell, we're like family already." Lloyd hugged her. "You be careful out there. If you need any manpower, let me know."

"I will." Her hair flared out in a brighter shade of red blond reacting to her attraction to him. "Thank you."

After Lloyd was gone, Jane reported the cash she'd taken in. "He had three hundred dollars in small bills."

"He probably picked that up as tips last night," she said. "And you were both worried for nothing. Lloyd understood that we have to make money too."

"It wasn't just that," Jane said softly. "He had to be warned, didn't he? This way he has a better chance of staying safe."

"Maybe so," Sunshine said. "But next time voice your opinion instead of looking at me like you're going to eat the paper."

"I only chewed on the first two," Jane told her. "I didn't chew on the one I gave him."

"I think our path is laid out before us," Aine said. "We should go to the tattoo establishment and search for clues that match the dumpster and the roof. Is that correct?"

"Absolutely. You're a fast learner for a fairy, even one that's been dead for a long time."

The beane sidhe rose to her feet, towering over her partner. "And you are not a bad person for a witch."

"Yeah. Thanks for that. I don't know what kind of witches you knew back in Ireland, but all my friends are like me."

"I doubt that." Aine accompanied her out of the small office.

Sunshine kept talking about the kind of witch she was as she told Jane they were leaving and to call if anything came up. They went out to the convertible, and she started the engine

"What do you know of Mr. Bad, as you call him?" Aine asked. "From whence did he hail, and for what length of time has he lived in this place?"

"He was here one morning. He said he was looking for the right place and wanted to stay." Sunshine glanced into her rearview mirror. "He's never been any trouble. We never even know he's there."

"But never leaves that room?"

"No. Never." Sunshine backed out of the parking lot. "Why do you ask?"

Aine's green gaze remained on the black road before them. "Have you no fear of him?"

"None at all." Sunshine glanced at her once they were in traffic. "Should I?"

"I'm certain if you needed to fear him, you would know."

"That's cryptic. Is there something you should tell me?"

Sunshine had always taken Mr. Bad's presence for granted. Why was Aine asking about him?

"No," Aine said. "I'm sure everything 'twill be fine."

It worried Sunshine as they drove down Granby Street from the historic district back to the tattoo shop. She had enough going on without wondering about Mr. Bad's motives. He was there. He was always there. She counted on that certainty. John had told her that she could trust him. That was good enough for her.

The police had completely cordoned off the area around *Tattoo Hell*. A large crowd had assembled outside to see what was going on. Cell phones were raised as cameras clicked. Local news crews had joined them. It was like a circus.

Aine started to get out of the car.

"Let's think about this." Sunshine surveyed the crowd. She could see O'Neill and Malto near the entrance. "We can't just walk in there. We have no authority, and I'd hate O'Neill's new good wishes for his *beane sidhe* to go to waste when his partner wants him to arrest us because of that video. We could go in with my invisibility spell. That way no one will see us."

"I would rather not be spelled," Aine said. "You go. I'll wait here."

"All right. Maybe I can find something to bring out with me for you to smell. That could be helpful if you could find the killer that way." Sunshine frowned. "You're okay, aren't you? Really, Aine, what happened with you and O'Neill this morning? Why did you change?"

"I cannot say. This time is strange for me. Things are happening that I cannot control."

"Well, you just hang in there. Let's try to keep it together until we find John's killer anyway. Then you can take some time off. Relax for a while. It doesn't look like O'Neill is gonna die anytime soon." Sunshine started to pat her hand but stopped herself. "I'll be right back."

Aine watched Sunshine become invisible—not to her but apparently to everyone else. The witch slipped into the building without anyone stopping her.

The idea of going back to Castle O'Neill to live out what time she had left on the earth alone crossed her mind. This city—this age—was so different than any other she'd experienced. She felt lost and uncertain.

She didn't understand why O'Neill's careless touch had made her change forms. Perhaps this was why the rule of never touching a *beane sidhe* was strictly adhered to. She didn't know why O'Neill had laid hands on her. She knew that it wasn't right and couldn't happen again.

That was when she heard the cry from somewhere around the building. She got out of the car to search the roofs around her. It had come from overhead. It wasn't human, and was fueled by ancient magic, as Mr. Bad had suggested.

Her keen eyes caught the flicker of a dark wing, but that was all. Silence followed, except for the noise from the city that she was growing accustomed to. She watched for a few more minutes to see if anything else appeared, but there was no sign of the creature she thought she'd seen.

"You!" Detective Malto said in an accusatory tone.

She left her place at the door to *Tattoo Hell* to cross the street, her eyes fastened on the distinctive purple convertible. "You've got some nerve turning up here. O'Neill was trying to convince me that you and blondie are just innocent bystanders in all this. And yet here you are again. You just couldn't stay away from what you did, could you?"

Her presence barely registered on Aine until the detective tried to put metal cuffs on her wrists.

"That's right. You look at me when I talk to you." Malto continued her tirade. "I'm taking you in whether O'Neill thinks it's a good idea or not."

Aine shook her hand, and the cuffs fell to the ground at her feet. "I do not seek to harm you, detective. Please go back to O'Neill and continue your investigation."

Malto pulled her service revolver and got up in her face. "On the ground, face down. I don't want to see you look up until I've told you your rights, you sick witch."

"Witch?" Aine was angered and confused by the detective referring to her this way. "I am certainly not a witch, young woman."

"You heard me," Malto persisted. "On the ground!"

"It is not I that shall fall before you." Aine's eyes flared brilliantly into Detective Malto's gaze. "Kneel. Put down that weapon."

Detective Malto dropped to her knees in the trashed concrete parking lot. She flung down her revolver. "How may I serve you, my lady?"

"That's better. I require nothing of you except that you work faithfully with O'Neill and ignore my presence. Do you understand?"

"Yes, my lady."

"Good."

O'Neill rushed across the street to join them. Horns blared as he skirted around oncoming traffic, flashing his badge. "What's going on? What did you do to her, Aine?"

"I did nothing. Detective Malto and I were having a conversation." Her tone was hard and cold. It was all she could do to keep from changing form into the old, gray hag.

He helped Malto to her feet, but she was still staring straight ahead as though his presence didn't register. "Sharon? Are you okay?"

"She is well, O'Neill. I would not harm her unless she was trying to harm you." Aine didn't understand his concern.

"I'm not sure what you mean by harming her, but stealing her brain isn't exactly a good thing. Let her go."

Aine nodded. "Surely."

Malto blinked. "Where did you come from?" she asked her partner.

"I was wondering why you were over here," he said. "We talked about leaving Sunshine Merryweather and Aine out of this."

"Yeah. Sure." Malto glared at Aine. "Let's get back to the crime scene."

O'Neill didn't follow her across the street right away. He stared into Aine's eyes. "You're supposed to obey me or something, right?"

She inclined her head.

"Well I'm giving you a direct command. Don't do anything to her again. Sharon Malto is my friend and partner. Leave her alone. If you have a problem with her, tell me. I'll handle it. Is that clear?"

"Of course, O'Neill."

He acted as though he was ready for an argument from her. When none came, it stole his thunder. He was left with only a closing remark. "Okay. Thanks."

Sunshine was quickly crossing the street to Aine as O'Neill was leaving. He looked right at her as though he'd seen her and then shook his head as he continued back to the tattoo shop.

"What was that all about?" Sunshine asked as she reappeared.

"Nothing," Aine said. "What did you find?"

Chapter Thirteen

Sunshine described the scene inside to Aine and took a piece of ripped and bloody t-shirt out of a bag. "Here. Smell this. See what you think. I think it's the same person."

"Perhaps not a person in the way that you mean it. I heard something out here while you were gone—I haven't heard such a sound since I was very young."

"So for a really, really long time. What was it?"

"I can't say for sure. I'm not certain if I actually saw one of the creature's black wings as it flew away."

"I get it," Sunshine said impatiently. "You're not one hundred percent on this. It's only a guess. Give it your best shot."

Aine's forehead furrowed as she tried to decipher her partner's words. "I am not familiar with that phrase."

"Geez! Just tell me what you think is doing this."

"A harpy."

Sunshine's eyes widened dramatically and her hair

curled tightly. "A what? Weren't they only around in Greek mythology?"

"When I was a child, a witch summoned one of the creatures to serve her. The harpy took the lives of several people before the witch was killed. They are usually called to take blood vengeance. Sometimes it can be justified—such as the murder of a loved one. Sometimes it is petty revenge for a real or perceived wrong against the summoner."

"Really?" Sunshine searched Aine's eyes before she started the car. "You're telling me that someone from Norfolk called up 1-800-Get-a-Harpy to take care of their problems. Is that even possible?"

"For the right practitioner. It would doubtless be a witch who is committed to the dark arts. The witch would have to do more than dabble to call and control a harpy. Do you know of such a witch?"

"Sure. I know of several powerful witches. But they aren't the kind you can call up and ask out for lunch." Sunshine started the car and careened out of the parking lot. "Lunch! I almost forgot. My aunt is in town today, and I promised to have lunch with her. You might as well come along, even if you don't eat. She's older—maybe she's seen a harpy too."

Sunshine drove quickly to the cafe where she had scheduled to meet her aunt. She took a quick look at her hair and makeup before she went in with Aine. She knew her aunt would tell her mother everything about her.

"Aunt Molly!" Sunshine found her and gave her a big hug. "You look great. I love that new necklace. Where did you find it?"

"It's actually quite old," Molly Addison Renard said of her large amulet. "It belonged to a very ancient witch in our family line. Since I don't have anyone with magic as a descendant to leave it to, you might be the one to inherit it."

"Thanks." Sunshine was about to touch it when she saw something move inside it. "What is that? Is something living in there?"

"I know that piece," Aine said. "I have seen it in a time long past. It once belonged to Mananan MacLir. How came you by it, witch?"

Molly laughed but her cornflower blue eyes were wary. She looked to be in her late fifties but being Sunshine's aunt made her older than her appearance. Her brown hair was attractively styled but in a subdued fashion. "Who's your new friend, Sunshine?"

The hostess told them a table was ready. They followed the young woman to a spot with a pretty pink tablecloth and flowers on it. A waitress came and took their order for drinks.

"Aunt Molly, this is Aine of Ulster. She's a real life *beane sidhe*. She came from Ireland searching for the last member of the family she serves."

Molly nodded at Aine, but kept one hand on the necklace. "Aine."

"Aine, this is my Aunt Molly. She's a water witch. She's fourth or fifth generation in my family line. She's from Wilmington, North Carolina."

Aine warily nodded back, knowing well the power of the magic held inside the other woman's necklace.

They faced each other across the pretty table as though they were about to battle.

"Really, ladies." Sunshine intervened. "I love this place. I don't want to be thrown out. Aunt Molly, Aine is a friend. We're working together at the agency. Aine, my aunt is not your enemy."

"I understand," Aine replied. "But the magic in that amulet is rarely held in a human's hand."

"It was passed down to me," Molly explained. "A sea god gave it to an ancestor of ours, and it came to me through the family line."

Aine nodded. "Ah. A gift from an immortal. Rare but not unheard of. Particularly from MacLir, who was always very generous with his lovers."

"Hold on a minute." Sunshine recapped. "That came from a sea god? Are they around too? I thought *beane sidhes* were gone, and now there are sea gods. I suppose harpies are possible too."

Molly moved her hand from her amulet, more relaxed now that she understood what was going on. "Harpies? You know a harpy?"

Sunshine picked up the wine list as their server returned. "I think I'm going to need something stronger than sweet tea to explain all this. Would anyone care to join me?"

It took most of lunch to acquaint Molly with everything that was going on, even as fast as Sunshine spoke. They had wonderful food and wine with lunch—at least Sunshine and Molly did. Aine didn't eat, although she did have a glass of wine. If the server heard anything of their unusual conversation, she didn't let on but kept the wine bottle close at hand.

"That's quite a story," Molly said to her niece. "Don't worry. I won't mention it to your mother. The last thing you need right now is for her to fly up here and try to tell you how to take care of it. You've done so well with your detective agency, Sunshine. I'm glad you found something you enjoy doing."

"Thanks. It can get hairy, but I really love it."

"What about Jane? Have you had any luck changing her back to a normal mouse?"

"No. But she's happy transforming into a woman when she feels like it," Sunshine said. "And she's a wiz on the computer."

Molly frowned. "But her permanent transformation isn't what the universe intended."

"Maybe not." Sunshine's smile was strained. "But I think she's happy. And if I can reverse the magic at some point, she'll have a choice about it. Until then, she has plenty to keep her busy."

"And fed," Aine observed.

Sunshine asked how things were going in Wilmington. Molly told her that she and her coven were doing well. "We've actually added two new witches. Brian is very strong, although not well trained. The other is Dorothy—she's actually Olivia's daughter. She wasn't raised a witch, but she's coming along very nicely."

"Olivia's daughter?" Sunshine wondered. "That must be a story!"

"It is. Imagine Olivia being able to keep a secret for so long!"

They laughed at that, and Sunshine asked after her Uncle Joe and her cousin, Mike, who had no magic. They were Molly's husband and son. Sunshine's mother was also married to a man who wasn't a witch.

"How's your boyfriend, John? Are you two still together?" Molly asked.

Sunshine got uncharacteristically quiet. "He's dead, Aunt Molly. He was murdered, maybe by the harpy."

"Murdered? I'm so sorry." Molly was shocked. "I'd offer your uncle's help with that investigation, but if there's a harpy involved, anyone without magic should stay far away. There's only so much a police detective can do."

"I know." Sunshine collected herself, putting it from her. Her eyes were red, but she kept the tears from falling. "I have Aine now. You can't go wrong with a *beane sidhe*, right?"

"I'm sure that's true." Molly squeezed her niece's hand. "Don't forget that we love you. Call if you get into trouble."

"I will." Sunshine sniffed but managed to keep it together.

Molly had to leave right after lunch. She was picking up her son at college on her way back to Wilmington. She hugged Sunshine again when it was time to go and smiled at Aine. "Good luck you two. Come visit when you get a chance. Aine, please come with her."

"Thank you," Aine replied gravely.

"Bye, Aunt Molly. Give Uncle Joe and Mike a hug for me."

"Are you the sea god's lover?" Aine abruptly asked before Molly could get in the car.

Molly's rosy complexion went deep red as she laughed. "Good heavens no! But my friend, Olivia may have had a dalliance with him. I try not to think about it."

Dark clouds swept over the city from the sea. Rain wasn't far. Small and mid-size boats were putting in to harbor as the wind rose and the barometer plummeted.

"When I first came here, I was immediately attracted to your purple door agency," Aine said as they got back in the car.

"Why do you think that was?"

"Power calls to power. I was drawn there as surely as I was pulled here by the presence of Sean O'Neill."

"I'm not that powerful." Sunshine laughed.

"No," Aine agreed. "But Mr. Bad is. His presence has made your detective agency as a beacon in the night to the creatures of magic and darkness."

Sunshine didn't know if she agreed with that, but she thought about it on the way back to the agency. When the *beane sidhe* had gone to check on O'Neill, Sunshine knocked on Mr. Bad's office door. Jane scampered away before he called to come in.

"Miss Merryweather," he said as she closed the door behind her. "Is there something I can do for you?"

"I wanted to tell you that Aine has a feeling about the killer who murdered John and the others."

"Yes?"

Did his voice sound worried? Was there something not quite the same about his tone? Sunshine considered it. Was he wondering if Aine had told her something about him that could ruin their relationship?

She explained about the two new deaths at the tattoo shop and the possibility that a harpy might be responsible.

"Do you have any experience with harpies? Is that even possible?"

He took a slow deep breath that seemed to make the room breathe around him. "You must know by now that anything is possible. It has been many years since I saw a *beane sidhe*. It would be much longer that I would have seen a harpy. But these creatures don't disappear, Miss Merryweather. They hide in places no one thinks to look for them until someone summons them—or they are needed once more."

"It's going to take some serious research to figure out how to get rid of a harpy."

"As I'm certain Aine has pointed out, you must search for the summoner." His chair squeaked as he moved in it. "I should advise strong caution. It would be unlikely that you would survive an encounter with a harpy."

"Yeah. You're probably right. Aine might be able to take on one of them."

"That's difficult to say."

"Well, thanks for your help." She stood to leave, her insides quaking before she asked the next question. "Aine says the agency acts as a beacon to creatures like this. What do you think?"

"I think Aine is an ancient who knows far more than she will admit. Be wary, Miss Merryweather. There is definitely danger ahead."

Sunshine thanked him again and left the dark office. She wished Aine had never made her think about Mr. Bad—who he was and why he was here in her building. Now she couldn't stop thinking about it and wanting to ask him. It could only lead to trouble.

"I got a hit on Amos Johnson," Jane told her when she had left Mr. Bad's office. "He's been admitted to the hospital. His condition is critical."

"Thanks," Sunshine said. "I'm going there right away. I'll call Lloyd as I go. When Aine gets back, send her there."

"I will," Jane promised. "Would it be okay if I take a few minutes for lunch? There's still plenty of cereal and nuts."

"Take whatever time you need," Sunshine said. "Just answer the phone if it rings."

"Okay." Jane nibbled on the side of a pencil. "I will."

"Not the pencil."

"Sorry." She put the pencil on the desk and went toward the kitchen.

Sunshine considered her aunt's words about Jane's life not being what nature intended. She knew it showed in her actions every day. She should've had a thousand mouse babies by now and none of the stress working in her office. She hadn't given up on trying to reverse that spell. It had eluded her so far, but she was determined to take care of it.

In the meantime, Aine was observing O'Neill having lunch with his girlfriend. The artist lived in a high rise with a huge window overlooking the blue water. Elena Spiros was indeed very beautiful—with wide enough hips to imagine her bearing at least one or two children. She wore her long, black hair loose on her shoulders and gazed lovingly into O'Neill's eyes.

"Here." He smiled as he held a tender morsel of chicken near Elena's brilliant red lips. "I know you must be hungry."

She leaned forward and kissed him. "Only for you, my love. We don't need food. It's enough that we have the nectar of the gods—love."

It was hard for Aine to listen to such tripe. She could not completely disappear as Sunshine could, but she could camouflage herself and blend in with any background. At that moment, she was standing against the ivory-colored wall behind O'Neill and his beloved.

The room was filled with Elena's paintings. There were landscapes, portraits, even a nude study of O'Neill. Aine looked at it as well as the other drawings and paintings of him. The O'Neills were always a handsome lot with plenty of charm that they spread abundantly with the people in their family as well as those who knew them casually.

"Are you sure you can't have some wine?" Elena didn't wait for an answer before filling his glass.

"No. Only coffee for me. I have to be back on duty again in a few minutes." He leaned close and kissed her. "But it's been a wonderful lunch. We should do this more often."

"Stay with me. Forget your job for once." She wrapped her arms around him so tightly that Aine feared she might be about to choke him. "What is it that keeps you doing what you do? Why would you put yourself in danger that way?"

"Someone has to do it," he said. "Why do you paint?"

"Because it expresses my soul." She bit his ear and then licked it. "Stay with me. Let someone else discover who killed those people."

"I don't think my partner would like that, Elena." He kissed her and then got to his feet from the blanket they'd shared on the floor. "Dinner tonight?"

She pouted. "Must I be a corpse to get any attention from you?"

"You get all my attention because you're so alive."

"I can't have dinner tonight with you. The gallery called. They're going to be exhibiting my paintings beginning next week. Can you come for that?"

"I'll be there as soon as I can. I can't wait to see the exhibit."

Aine followed him out of the apartment. She was careful not to let him see her. It seemed earlier that he'd glimpsed Sunshine while she was spelled to be invisible. The O'Neills had never had the sight, but perhaps this one was different.

She got off the elevator with him. Shards of lightning were beginning to fragment the sky as rain started falling in large drops, the breeze bringing the smell of wet pavement to her nostrils.

Because she was so intent on following him without being seen, she almost didn't realize it when she suddenly appeared before him in the courtyard. The space was empty except for them, set behind a large wood fence that separated them from the busy street.

"O'Neill." Her voice was hoarse and deep. The gray cerements of her burial shroud surrounded her, fluttering in the strong breeze. She was the hag again and realized she was bringing him news which she hadn't foreseen. "This is the first warning of your death."

Chapter Fourteen

O'Neill took a quick step back from her gaunt face and dark eye sockets. "Aine?"

"You cannot outrun your doom, young O'Neill. Your death is at hand."

The warning was ripped from her, torn from what soul remained in her. It had never happened this way—no warning to her at all—even though in the past she had been close with the other O'Neills whose deaths she had forewarned. This time it was as though her intentions were not her own. She had changed form again without wishing for it.

It was wrong, and yet she couldn't control it. The first of three warnings had been issued. She wailed loudly, bemoaning O'Neill's impending demise, as was her duty. He stared at her, unblinking, in his terror.

Aine didn't bother to resume her middle-aged form clothed in black. She let the storm winds lift and carry her away from the spot in the pleasant courtyard. She was not human any longer after all, having been dead herself more years than she could remember. The storm carried her back to the red brick building with the purple door. Inside, she went to her room and collapsed on the floor in tears.

She wasn't sure if she was more amazed at the death warning that had come over her without thought or knowledge—or if the tears that slid down her face were more astonishing. The last time she could remember crying was at the death of her infant son. She had been alive at that time, still the warrior Queen of Ulster. She'd hidden her tears from her army, lest they think her weak.

Why was she crying for O'Neill? How many of the family had she seen die? More than she could count, down through the centuries. This was why she'd been called here. This was why she'd awakened. Her job now was to give O'Neill two more warnings before his death. Then she would be there to comfort him as he died and escort his soul to the underworld.

Aine would be free of her curse at that time. The last O'Neill would be gone with no heir to carry on his bloodline. It was good. It was right. Her penance would be done. She would fall to dust, her life behind her.

There was a tiny knock at the door. "I'm sorry to bother you." Jane's voice was barely audible. "I saw you come in and wanted to be sure you were okay."

The tremor in her tone made Aine realize what strength it took from this most pitiful creature to approach her this way. She forced herself to take on the middle-aged human form before she opened the door.

Jane was still a woman but barely holding on to that image. Her nose twitched and eyes bulged. Terror was written on every aspect of her countenance.

Because Aine respected the mouse's courage, she was gentle with her. "I am as I have been. Go back to your duties. There is nothing you can do for me."

"All right. I-I just wanted to check on you."

Aine managed a smile. "You have the bravery of a lion, child. Warriors have trembled when they spoke to me and would not have done so if they were not forced. Carry it proudly."

"Thanks."

Jane crept away from the door. Aine went back into the room to stare at the city around her from the window. A short while later, Sunshine was there with a more insistent knock.

"Where were you?" She opened the door before Aine could answer. "I waited at the hospital for you."

"I had matters of my own to settle."

Sunshine sat on the bed. "What happened? Did you catch O'Neill with his lover or something?"

"I observed the two as they shared a repast."

"Not sure what that is, but it doesn't sound all that great. Are you in love with O'Neill? Before you answer, I know you're not supposed to be. I've read everything I can find on *beane sidhes*. You don't fall in love with the ones you serve. You just take them away when they're dead. But this one is different, isn't he?"

Aine remained at the window. "Once long ago, I did love one of the O'Neill men." She thought about the miniature portrait. "I believe he loved me too. But it could only end in heartbreak. I am not a woman of flesh and blood any longer. When he died, and I left him in the underworld, a part of me stayed there with him. It made what came after harder to bear."

"So you can fall in love with them, but it's really stupid because you keep going. I get it. I've fallen for some normal humans too. We have to love where and when we can, Aine. We aren't ordinary women. It will never be easy for us."

"I had to announce O'Neill's death to him today."

"What? He's dying?"

"At this time he is well and healthy. I can only assume his premature death comes from his investigation into this case or another. I cannot see into the future. It may be the harpy that takes his life."

Sunshine bounded off the bed. "All the more reason we need to take out this creature. Between us it should be a snap. We're as big and awesome as women can be."

Aine thought about her conversation with Mr. Bad. "A harpy may be impossible for us to slay."

"Maybe." Sunshine repeated her words. "We're strong together. We can take her. Did you warn O'Neill?"

"Of his death."

"Did you mention how he might die? He could protect himself. There's a big difference between getting shot by some punk in the street and being ripped apart by a harpy."

"No. It is not my place to give him notions of how he might die."

"Or what? You burst into flames? The earth swallows you?"

Aine held her hands tightly together. The witch was starting to anger her. She resisted changing form into the crone. "It is not allowed. There are rules."

"And you gave him warning of his death. Does that mean he has to die? Have you ever warned one of the O'Neills and something changed so that he didn't die?"

"Yes, but—"

"So there you go. We have to see him and tell him what we suspect. Maybe he could start wearing protective gear. At least he'd have a fighting chance. Or are you just happy it will be over when he dies?"

An immediate change came over Aine. The room around them shook with it. The force of her transformation shattered the mirrors and the glass in the window she'd been looking out of.

"Don't you imagine I want to save him?" Her voice was like nothing human as it came from her skeletal form. "I would help if I could. Being with him is all that matters. There is nothing left for me when he dies."

Aine didn't realize until the rage left her that she was grasping Sunshine by her plump, white throat and shaking the breath from her. As she came back to herself, she released her, praying she hadn't taken her life. Sunshine dropped to the carpet and dissolved into it. Puzzled, Aine pushed at the floor with her foot.

"Over here." Sunshine whistled to draw her attention. "I told you I read all about the *beane sidhe*—including that they have a bad temper and little use for humans not in the family they serve."

"You tricked me."

"Sort of." Sunshine grinned. "Better that than Jane running up here trying to get revenge because you killed me."

The image of the mouse attempting to avenge the witch made Aine laugh. It hadn't happened in so long that she choked on it, and her form changed to the young queen. Rosy-cheeked and pink of flesh, she continued to bubble with merriment.

"All right," Sunshine said. "That's gotta put you in a better mood."

The laughter slowly died, but the young queen's regal beauty remained. "It is forbidden for me to tell O'Neill how he might meet his death. To do so could mean he and I would both wander the earth forever without peace. I would not wish that for him."

"But I'm not governed by those rules." Sunshine stared deeply into her bright eyes. "I'll tell him about the harpy. Let's save him now instead of mourning him when he's gone. We can kick this harpy out of our town. Don't give up so soon."

Aine had never felt as strong a bond as she did with this woman that she had only known a few days. She knew the pain behind the brilliant blue eyes that stared into hers. She could feel the strong magic in the witch.

Slowly she nodded as her form reverted to the middle-aged woman in black. "You are wise beyond your years, Sunshine Merryweather. Let us vanquish our foe and show no mercy. I swear my allegiance in this matter to our cause."

"Awesome! Then let me tell you what I learned at the hospital as we look for O'Neill."

Sunshine told Jane to take the rest of the day off as they headed out to the car.

"Lloyd met me at the hospital," she told Aine. "We sneaked in to see Amos. He was barely alive. I haven't had a chance to research harpies yet, but I saw the claw marks all over him. She nearly scratched him to pieces. Some man came into the alley where she was attacking him, and she flew away."

"Flew away?"

"Yeah. That's what I thought too. The big, bad harpy of ancient mythology just takes off if someone sees her at work. Does that sound right to you?"

"No. Harpies have no thought of self. They do what they are sent to do. She should have finished killing Amos and probably killed the man who interrupted her."

"Why didn't she?" Sunshine pondered. "This way she left Amos alive to tell people about her."

"Is there a knight protecting the lad at the hospital?"

Sunshine made a quick U-turn in the street. "I don't think so. We better find out."

They drove to the hospital. Its stark cleanliness and white walls amazed Aine as they rushed inside. They ran by O'Neill and Malto in their haste to reach the elevator.

"Hey," Malto called out. "What are you two doing here?"

O'Neill couldn't make eye contact with Aine as they got in the elevator with them.

"We're here to save Amos Johnson's life," Sunshine said.

"He just woke up," O'Neill told her. "We're on our way to question him. There's an officer stationed outside his door.

He's in no danger now."

"You won't mind if we ride up to confirm that with you, right?" Sunshine's blue eyes were steely.

"Who are these women, O'Neill?" Malto demanded. "Why do they keep following us around?" But her eyes never reached Aine's gaze.

"I'm a licensed private detective." Sunshine fished around in her bag until she found her ID and then flashed it at them. "We're working a case just like you."

"Except that you have no authority to be here."

"It doesn't matter if they go up with us." O'Neill ended the discussion. "But not in the room, Merryweather. It ends at the door."

Sunshine agreed only a moment before the elevator doors parted. The two teams quickly left the conveyance, headed for the same hospital room.

O'Neill took a deep breath when he saw the officer still stationed outside the door. "Everything okay here?"

The officer got to his feet. "Yes, sir. No one in or out, just like you said."

Malto turned to push open the hospital room door with a supreme expression of righteousness. "That's it for you, ladies. We'll take it from here."

Her manner changed abruptly when the open door revealed an empty room with blood-splattered walls.

"The window." Aine rushed toward it. The glass had been broken from the outside, but there was telltale evidence that someone had been dragged out of it. Bits of flesh and green hospital garb clung to the fractured edges.

Malto dared to look over her shoulder. "That's not possible. This room is eight floors up. The wall is smooth. There's nothing to climb on."

Aine removed a single feather from the window pane. "I wish that were so."

Chapter Fifteen

Malto and O'Neill were immediately on their phones summoning help from the police department.

"He can't have gotten too far," Malto told her partner. "Even if he had suction cups for feet and climbed up here to snatch Johnson. He still had to get away with him."

A cup of coffee dropped and burst on the floor behind them. "What the hell happened here?" Lloyd asked. "Where's Amos?"

"I'm sorry, sir." Malto escorted him out of the room. She put the officer stationed outside the door to work gathering security guards to search the hospital.

"Tell him," Sunshine urged Aine when they were alone with O'Neill.

"You said you were going to tell him," she replied with trepidation as she glanced at him.

He looked away. "Tell me what? What's going on?"

Sunshine stepped hard on Aine's slippered foot. "Tell him for goodness sake."

Aine angrily glanced up to yell at Sunshine but found herself gazing into O'Neill's questioning eyes.

"Tell me," he urged. "I guess there aren't any other secrets between us, right? Tell me the truth."

"Your killer is a harpy," Aine explained. "She is most likely thousands of years old. She does not kill for sport. If she's here, someone summoned her to kill for them."

O'Neill blinked. "A harpy? You mean like in the movies—kind of like a woman with wings and sharp claws. That kind of harpy?"

"Yes." Aine was surprisingly relieved to tell him the truth. "She is cunning and devious. No doubt it is her presence which caused me to warn you of your death."

He stared at her for a moment. "About that. You were in the apartment with me and Elena, weren't you?"

"Yes."

"I guess having your own *beane sidhe* means having no privacy. Is that about right?"

"Yes," she admitted. "What good is my sworn duty to take you to the underworld at the moment of your death if I am not present at that moment?"

"Okay. Let's just put that aside for now. I can't handle that and what's happened here at the same time. I can't believe I'm asking this, but what makes you think a harpy is killing people?"

Aine gave him the feather she'd found. "Observe this, O'Neill. It is one of the harpy's feathers yet unlike any feather you have ever seen."

He took it between his fingers. "It feels more like metal. Are you sure it's real?"

"Is Amos Johnson still here attached to an IV?" Sunshine asked. "Snap out of it. You have a *beane sidhe* that you've seen in full *beane sidhe* mode. There are other things in the world that you don't know about. You have to protect yourself and find some way to tell your obnoxious partner that she could be in danger too."

"Saying it's real, how do we find this thing?" He studied the feather. "I'm giving this to forensics."

"We must follow the trail of the kill," Aine said. "They are not secretive predators. We should find remnants of Amos Johnson as we track her."

"We don't have time for forensics," Sunshine explained. "We have a list of possible targets for the harpy. Amos was one of them. Our friend in the other room might be another."

She explained what they knew about the killings. O'Neill listened carefully, ignoring the chaos going on outside the door.

"So you think the harpy was sent to kill John Lancaster and Amos Johnson but took it on herself for whatever reason to kill Harley Matthews and the other two at the tattoo shop."

"That's what we think." Sunshine glanced at Aine who'd been quiet throughout her explanation. "Of course we have an expert on harpies and all things ancient with Aine here. She's been around since dirt too. If *beane sidhes* are possible, anything is."

"But if the harpy only kills what she's sent to kill," O'Neill added, "why kill the other men?"

"They were helping her find the ones she wanted to kill, but they got greedy and wanted more money. She wasn't willing to share."

"The creature cares nothing for gold or fame," Aine finally said. "She is bound by unbreakable law to finish the task her master has set. You must understand the needs of the master to understand why the harpy kills."

"And how do we find the master?" O'Neill asked.

"I have already explained to Sunshine that we must locate a strong, dark witch who would be capable of summoning such a creature."

"And now we're looking for witches *and* a harpy." He shook his head. Malto called sharply for him. "I gotta go. I don't know what to say about all this. I'm not really good with things I can't see or touch."

He left them to find Malto.

"It was useless telling him the truth," Aine said. "He doesn't believe."

"He does believe part of it—you. He knows you exist. It won't be that big a stretch for him to believe the rest. In the meantime, he's been warned. Maybe he can use that to his advantage. You and I have a visit to pay to the worst witch in the city, at least that I know of."

"Are you not afraid of this witch?"

"Not with you around." Sunshine grinned. "Besides, she's kind of old and probably isn't as strong as she used to be. But just in case, you're my ace in the hole."

They walked through the hospital corridor as more police officers poured through the hallways, radios squawking.

"How will you locate this witch?" Aine asked as they got in the elevator.

"Piece of cake," Sunshine bragged. "It's not like she tries to hide. We'll just go knock on her door. Briana will see us when she takes a look at you."

The elevator dropped to the ground floor and the doors opened. But they weren't at the hospital lobby. Instead, there were several women in red gowns waiting for them in a room filled with antiques and protective sigils which was backed by red brocade walls. The pungent smell of burning sage was thick in the air.

The red-gowned women bowed to them as one. "She will see you now."

Sunshine tried not to appear nervous. "You see. I told you it would be easy to find her."

The five women became a guard around them as they walked down a long hall. One woman was in front and one behind them. The other three stayed at their sides. The hall seemed to go on forever. It finally came to an abrupt end as it became a cavernous red space. No walls or ceiling were visible.

A woman was seated at the center of it. She was completely dressed in white. Her hair was also white, but her eyes were black.

"Hello, Sunshine." She smiled as she said it. "I haven't seen or heard from you in a very long time. How is your aunt? I understand she was here for a visit recently."

"Hello, Briana. Aunt Molly is doing well. I can't recall the last time you and I spoke." Sunshine raised her brows. "Oh wait. I remember now—it was the day you tried to kill me."

"Surely that's all water under the bridge. All things have been forgiven and forgotten between us." Briana's gaze flicked toward Aine. "Who's your new friend?"

"This is Aine of Ulster. She's here for a visit. Maybe the two of you have run into each other at some point in the last few hundred years." Sunshine relished trying to provoke the other witch.

"Your majesty." Briana respectfully inclined her head. "I believe we have met before. How are you faring these days? The world has changed since last you glimpsed it."

Aine could feel the witch's power. Her magic was strong. Her words about having met before rang true. She didn't recognize Briana, but she remembered something about her. It was fleeting and old, gone before she could capture it.

"Greetings, Briana," Aine replied respectfully. "I think we have met. Your magic feels familiar to me."

Briana's lips were bright red in her face. "What brings you here, my lady? Surely you don't belong. Where is the O'Neill that you serve?"

"Let me answer that," Sunshine interrupted, afraid that Aine might go *beane sidhe* on the other woman before they got answers to their questions. "We're here about the harpy. Know anything about it?"

"A harpy?" Briana gave nothing away. "Here in Norfolk? I haven't heard anything about it. But what an intriguing idea."

"It's killed some shifters and a werewolf," Sunshine said. "It might be hunting any kind of magical creature. I'd hate to think it would come after you."

"I'm sure you would, dear. But you needn't worry. I can take care of myself, as you well know."

Sunshine took a step toward her. The five red women moved to defend their mistress.

Aine's middle-aged form changed to that of the boney crone in gray rags. "If we find you are aiding the harpy, we shall return, Briana. I am capable of more than simply serving O'Neill."

Her voice shook the room around them, causing fear and panic in the red women.

Briana still appeared unmoved by her threat. "I would expect nothing less."

"Now might be a good time to leave," Sunshine muttered to Aine. "I think you made our point."

Aine returned to her black garb. "She is not telling us the truth. She knows about the harpy."

"But only because we told her," Sunshine replied. "I'm willing to bet she's behind the eight ball on this."

They got back in the elevator, and Sunshine pressed the button for the ground floor, hoping they didn't end up smashed against it when they got there. Briana was capable of anything.

"You have the most peculiar manner of expression," Aine told her. "What is an eight ball?"

The elevator made a chiming sound, and the doors parted on the lobby floor of the hospital.

Sunshine took a deep breath of relief. "Thank the goddess."

"Briana is quite powerful," Aine said. "That was a fascinating display."

"She's got some mojo happening. But a lot of it is just bells and whistles." Sunshine grinned and couldn't resist hugging her companion. "Sorry. I know it's against the rules, but I'm really happy to be alive. Mr. Bad was right about you. You're tough."

Aine shrugged off the hug—now the second time someone had dared touch her in hundreds of years—yet within one day of each.

"But I see you didn't go all soft and pretty for me," Sunshine observed. "I think there's something else going on that you don't want to share."

Aine's gaze was fierce. "Shall we return to finding the harpy now?"

"Yes. Absolutely. Blood trail, right? O'Neill is probably already on it."

"All the more reason for us to follow. O'Neill does not comprehend what he is facing. He needs protection from his eagerness to find the truth."

"In other words, you're not just going to sit back and let him die because you sang his death song. Talk about somebody who has a weird way of saying things."

It was easy to pick up the blood trail. Sunshine had been ready to use magic to locate it, but Aine was right. It was in plain sight, dotting the sidewalks and the ground as the harpy flew through the city. People walked around or through it, not noticing the red droplets as they continued on their way.

"There's no way poor Amos survived this in the shape he was in," Sunshine said.

"It's curious that she didn't rip him to pieces where she found him." Aine kept her sharp eyes on the trail.

"Maybe we disturbed her. Maybe she was afraid of getting caught."

"This creature has no fear," Aine told her. "Something here is not as it should be. We don't understand as yet, but we will."

It was easy to discover where the harpy had finally left

Amos a few blocks away. By the time Aine and Sunshine reached the scene, O'Neill and Malto had already put up a police perimeter around a bloody dumpster in an alley.

"Guess that side trip to Briana's place cost us some time," Sunshine said as they watched other police vehicles arrive.

O'Neill looked up sharply before they reached him. His back was turned to them, but he seemed to sense her presence. Aine was pleased. Their relationship was odd, and certainly nothing like she'd experienced in the past with his ancestors, but they were coming to an understanding.

He approached them, leaving Malto behind to deal with the crime scene. "You were right. The harpy didn't try to hide. We followed it right here where she left Amos torn to pieces in the dumpster. What is this thing, and why is it here?"

Sunshine took out her phone, Googled harpy, and read aloud: "*A mythical creature with the head and torso of a woman whose razor-like talons and teeth exacted revenge on wrongdoers.*"

"Thanks. I could've done that." He didn't avoid Aine's gaze this time. "Let's say I believe there are witches, *beane sidhes*, harpies, and other mythical creatures in the city. Why would this thing want to kill a bunch of guys and their customers at a tattoo shop?"

"An excellent question, O'Neill," Aine said. "We have been assured by the most powerful witch my partner knows that she did not summon the harpy."

"And you believe her?" he asked.

"I believe her as far as it goes," Sunshine said. "That doesn't mean she won't try to find some way to use the harpy herself now that she knows about it."

"What about you give me her name and number and I'll pay her a visit so I can come to my own conclusions on what she knows or doesn't know."

Sunshine laughed at him. "I don't think you really want

to do that. Let's just say I'm not giving you her name for your own benefit. Aine already told me you got one warning. Let's not go for two."

O'Neill glanced back at his partner. "I can't just take your word for these things. I'm not saying you're wrong—you obviously have some idea what you're talking about—however crazy that might be. But I need real proof to take back to my captain."

"You have the harpy's feather," Aine told him. "Take that and the Google to him. Let him make of it what he will."

"A harpy?" Briana gave nothing away. "Here in Norfolk? I haven't heard anything about it. But what an intriguing idea."

Chapter Sixteen

Sunshine and Aine spent the rest of the day looking for the shifters the harpy might still be tracking. They followed Sunshine's locator spells but couldn't pinpoint them.

"I don't know what else to do," Sunshine admitted. "Shifters can be difficult, especially if they don't want to be found. I guess they're on their own."

"What about the wolf?" Aine asked as a damp dusk began falling across the city.

"Marcus was good friends with John. Maybe if we go to some of John's favorite spots we'll run into him."

They went back to the agency to make sure everything was all right. Jane wasn't answering the phone, and Sunshine was worried about her.

"Are you afraid Briana might do her harm?"

"Not really. She knows where I live but my perimeter wards are strong. If she's looking for trouble she'll try to find me away from the agency."

"Why did she previously attempt to kill you?" Aine wondered.

"It was a miscommunication. Briana thought I was trying to take her man from her. I was with someone else. I could understand why she'd feel insecure—there's no comparison between us but really—older vampires aren't my thing. I could hardly believe she was willing to fight over him."

Aine nodded but didn't say anything.

"What? Didn't women fight over men in your time?"

"Frequently. And men fought over them. Many things remain the same throughout the ages."

They went inside the purple door, and the office was strangely quiet. Usually the instant the door opened, Jane was there with information or just to welcome them back. There was no sign of her.

Sunshine called for her. Aine watched the floor in case the girl was a mouse. She was about to suggest they ask Mr. Bad when Jane came running out of the kitchen area.

"I'm so sorry." The words were muffled as Jane tried to speak over the enormous amount of cereal she'd shoved in her mouth. "I was really nervous, and that made me really hungry."

"We talked about hoarding," Sunshine reminded her. "You don't have to store reserve food in your cheeks. You won't ever go hungry here."

"I know. But it was one of the first things my mother taught me." Cereal sprayed from her mouth as she continued speaking. A large tear rolled down her cheek.

"It's all right." Sunshine hugged her. "You can't help what you are. Don't worry about it. I'll get more cereal."

"Thank you. Is it all right if I go off duty now?"

"Sure. I'm not expecting anyone else tonight. Just relax. Let your tail out."

"Oh! One thing. Marcus Fletcher called and said he'd meet you at the club. He didn't say the name of the club or why he wanted to meet you. Werewolves are so quick to anger."

"Great. Thanks, Jane." Sunshine glanced at Aine. "Sounds like our next meetup."

But Aine felt pulled to be with O'Neill. "I must leave you, but I shall find you after I see to his needs."

"He's not dying, is he? You said there would be two more warnings."

Aine transformed into the hag wearing her burial shroud. "I pray this is not one of them."

"I can go with you," Sunshine offered. But Aine was already gone. "Okay then. I guess I'll change clothes and see what Marcus has to say."

"Do you need my help?" Jane asked.

"No, sweetie. You just take it easy. I'll be back soon."

* * *

Aine let the night breezes carry her across the crowded city. There were thousands of lights illuminating the darkness around her. A million voices were raised in conversation, calls for help, or whispered soft words of love. She heard them all as she passed with only one goal in mind—finding O'Neill.

As she felt his presence close at hand, she heard a series of loud pops. She realized it was the sound of weapon fire.

O'Neill was on the ground in a side street where the lights had been shot out. Malto was at his side with a dozen other police officers in uniform. They were firing at a group of men that were hiding behind a burned out car. The men had O'Neill and the officers pinned down with loud gunfire.

"Why are you not heeding my warning, O'Neill?" Aine appeared only to him.

He cringed away when he first saw her and then managed to relax and focus on the men who were firing at him again. "Why are you here? Am I going to die?"

"How the hell should I know?" Malto shouted back at him. "Get yourself a psychic or something. Right now let's figure out how to get those guys to stop shooting at us."

"Sorry," he said to his partner. "Go away," he told Aine. "I don't need your help to do my job."

"You continue to put your life in jeopardy." Aine looked at the people around him. One of the officers had already been hit and was bleeding from the arm.

"That's my job," he explained. "We stop the bad guys. Not all of them are harpies."

"But these 'bad guys' are simple to remove," she observed.

"Yeah? Well, why don't you remove them?"

"With great pleasure."

Aine rose quickly through the night that sheltered the criminals who waited behind the car. She allowed all of them to see her as she sounded a warning to them that she was there to protect O'Neill. The men, who'd recently robbed a jewelry store and shot two security guards, took one look at her, covered their ears, and ran directly into the line of fire between them and the police.

They were shrieking about the flying corpse they'd seen as the police put handcuffs on them. The men were quickly loaded into vehicles as the ambulance arrived for the officer who'd been shot.

Returning to O'Neill's side, Aine resumed her form as the middle-aged woman. He told Malto he had to take a phone call and let her handle the arrests while he signaled to Aine that she should follow him a short walk away.

"That's not what I meant," he whispered with a quick glance at his partner.

Aine was confused. "You said to remove them if I was able."

"I was being sarcastic." He shook his head. "Don't they have sarcasm where you come from?"

"Your life was in danger. It is my job to protect you or guide your way to the underworld."

"You can't save me every time someone shoots at me. I know why you're here, and I appreciate that you're doing your duty. But if it's all the same to you, it would be better if you found someone else to do it with."

"You are refusing my help?"

"Yes. I am refusing your help if that means I can live a normal life again. There must be someone else you can take care of, Aine. I release you from your debt to my family."

"If only it were that simple." She smiled sadly. "There is nowhere else for me to go but the grave, O'Neill. I am here for you whether you require it or not. There were others who wanted to do without me. My penance is clear and cannot be avoided."

"Gun!" Malto yelled out as one of the thieves they were processing grabbed a gun from the officer trying to put him in a car.

The man looked around desperately before plunging through the line of officers and heading in O'Neill's direction.

"Look out!" O'Neill yell at Aine as the escaped criminal came up behind her. He pushed her to one side and confronted the other man.

"No. I'm not going back in." He jerked the gun up to fire at O'Neill.

Aine immediately moved between them. The gunman shot her twice before O'Neill knocked him on the ground.

"Are you okay?" Malto asked O'Neill. When he nodded, she turned on him angrily. "What's so important that you have to deal with it during a bust?"

"I can't explain. Will you just take him?" O'Neill handed the man off to her and two officers. "I'll be right there." He turned back to Aine who'd shown no sign of being hit by the bullets. "Are you okay?"

"I am already of the grave. You do not need to worry about me." She handed him the bullets.

He stared into her face. "I'm sorry you have to do this. I wish there was another way. But thanks for your help."

She regally nodded to him. "I am here for you until the end."

"Yeah. I get it." He went to help his partner and glanced back, but Aine was gone.

He couldn't see her. She had camouflaged herself easily hiding in the shadows as the arrest proceeded and was finally over. She followed him as he went off duty and ended the night at Elena's gallery exhibit and finally in her bed.

Aine left him at that point, refusing to consider that she didn't want to see their lovemaking. She'd watched many of the O'Neills with their wives and mistresses. She had never felt sorrow or jealousy.

That wasn't the case with this O'Neill. Perhaps it was because he was the last. It could even be because she had been asleep for so long. She hoped that would change as their relationship continued. It was not her place to have those emotions for him. She wasn't meant to have feelings at all, not anymore.

Finding Sunshine was simple enough as she sought the witch through the streets of the city. She heard her laugh and smelled her perfume long before she saw her sitting at a table in a crowded room. She wasn't alone at the table—a wolf sat with her. Loud music and flashing lights surrounded them.

Aine would have left them there but for Sunshine's demeanor. She might not acknowledge it, but the witch was afraid. As she spoke to the wolf in muted tones, Aine sat in an empty chair at their table.

"Hey!" The wolf glanced up, surprised and wary. "Who are you?"

"This is my new partner. Aine, Marcus. And so forth." Sunshine frowned. "I'm glad you finally got here. Marcus has an idea where we can find the harpy."

Chapter Seventeen

Aine glanced around the crowded nightclub. "I can imagine this would be a perfect hiding place. No one would think to look for her here."

"No, not here. This is where John and I used to hang out. But I think I know where she is." He explained that he'd seen something odd the night John had died. "It wasn't just what I saw. It was a weird feeling. I smelled something strange too. I've never smelled anything like it."

"What did it smell like?" Sunshine asked.

"Death. That's all I can say. I knew someone was gonna die." He went back through the night John was killed. "We parted on the corner. He said he was going to see you, Sunshine. I was headed to a shifter club across town that stays open all night. As I walked away, I heard the sound, and my whole body shivered. It was like wings in the darkness. I couldn't see them, but I felt them."

"Yet you did not see Sunshine's lover killed by the

harpy?" Aine asked.

"Just call him John," Sunshine muttered.

"No. I heard about it the next day." Marcus rubbed his hands nervously on his dirty jeans. "I gotta tell you—I've been staying out of the way. John was stronger than me. I know what happened to him. I've been scared it would happen to me."

"Can you think of any reason someone would want to hurt you or John?" Sunshine asked.

"Only the obvious," he said. "Not everyone likes having werewolves around. They don't like shifters either. But why kill excellent tattoo artists? Was it just because they worked with us? I don't know."

"I don't think the harpy is here to purge Norfolk of shifters and werewolves," Sunshine said. "There has to be another reason."

He shrugged. "Maybe, but I don't know what it is. I'm thinking about getting out of town until it's safe again. I heard about Amos Johnson too."

"What similarities did these men possess?" Aine asked. "Was there anything between them that could link them to the harpy or the person who controls her?"

"I don't know." Marcus appeared to be getting more nervous by the moment as he kept surveying the crowd of dancers in the club. "I hope you'll let me know if you hear anything."

"Sure," Sunshine agreed. "Maybe you should get out of town. If John wouldn't have been here, he might still be alive."

"Not a bad idea." He got slowly to his feet, checking the area around him. "I'll catch you later. Watch out for that harpy thing. It's bad."

After he'd gone, Sunshine finished her drink as though she had nothing else to do.

"I have never encountered such a timid werewolf," Aine said.

"If they want to live in society, they can't be as wild as they used to be."

"A werewolf could at least give a harpy a good fight—not that werewolf, but a fierce one. I have seen one almost conquer."

"I imagine John gave her a good fight." Sunshine's curls were nearly flat against her head, and her eyes held unshed tears. "But he's dead the same as Amos and the men from the tattoo shop."

"A good fight only means a fast death sometimes," Aine said. "I'm sure your werewolf did what he could. Very few creatures can match a harpy for speed and ferocity."

"Let's get out of here." Sunshine got to her feet. "The music sucks."

Aine followed her without discussion. It was obvious that the witch was in pain. She knew there was no solace for that anguish. Only time could heal that wound.

They circled their way past the dancers and the band to reach the door. Neither one spoke as they reached the cool night air. A murder of crows flew up from the rooftops and screeched across the rising moon.

"Look there!" Aine pointed to a form flying above them.

Sunshine looked up and muttered a spell for sight. The darkness cleared for her. She was able to see a creature the size of a human with a woman's face and short wings. The top of the body was female with bare breasts, but the bottom was large bird legs that ended in sharp talons. Her hands were clawed as well.

She flew with purpose—fast and in a single direction—through the crows. Her face was twisted in the moonlight, her eyes forward facing, not even glancing at the birds she flew through. They held no interest for her.

"I'm going after her." Sunshine flew up, following the harpy. Her blue dress billowed in the air as she disappeared into the darkness.

"Not alone." Aine's body blended with the air currents

as she followed her partner. She couldn't see Sunshine or the harpy at first. They had already traveled quickly across the city. Aine looked down at the lights and the ocean, white-capped, near them. Then she heard the cry of the harpy as it found its prey and dropped down to the streets and buildings below it.

She wished for a weapon, any weapon. She also wished that Sunshine had waited until they were ready to face the creature together. She had never met a woman as headstrong and impulsive as the witch who'd casually adopted her into her life. Even when Aine was a young warrior queen, she understood the need for strategy when trying to defeat an enemy. And yet here she was, more than a thousand years later, following Sunshine, who knew nothing of warfare or strategy.

She didn't fear for herself—she was long dead and past fear of that kind. The fear that raced through her was for the witch. It surprised her because she had only experienced emotions for the O'Neills since she'd been doomed to serve them. Her newfound feelings for the talkative woman who loved purple were almost unsettling. Why would she bond with her?

"Down there!" Sunshine was beside Aine as they followed the harpy. The air currents rippled through her hair and caused her dress to wave like a flag on a windy day.

"I see her," Aine replied. "There is no way to defeat her without preparation. We must not follow this path."

"Go back then," Sunshine replied coldly. "I made a vow to kill this thing. I'm not stopping now that I finally found her."

Aine wouldn't abandon her new friend. She plummeted with her until they reached the street. She could smell the harpy—and something more—blood.

"She's gotta be here somewhere," Sunshine said. "She doesn't turn invisible, does she?"

"No. Not to my knowledge."

"Then all we have to do is follow that stench."

They followed their noses to a small park and searched for the harpy. Everything was so quiet. Not a bird called. No breeze fluttered through the dark trees.

Aine saw the creature first. She was bent over her prey, devouring what she could of it as she shredded the body. She knew from the scent that it was the werewolf they'd met at the bar.

"I command you to stop." Sunshine had seen her too. She created a strong spell and threw it at the creature.

The harpy barely glanced up and growled at her. She returned to her feasting without care.

"Spells won't work against her," Aine whispered. "She was born of ancient magic. Nothing today can affect her."

"We'll see about that." Sunshine closed her eyes and drew power to her like a lightning rod. It lit up her eyes and made her hair stand straight out from her head as though she'd grasped a high voltage wire. When she was ready, she targeted the creature with that energy. It burned across the space between them, lighting up the darkness.

The creature felt the blast of magic as well as the hatred and anguish behind it. She stopped eating. "Go away. If you seek death, it shall come for you later. Do not challenge me. You cannot defeat me with your pretty spells."

Aine expected her partner to come up with a stronger incantation since the harpy didn't move after its threat.

Instead Sunshine screamed and launched herself bodily at the creature. Her body had turned to silver, glowing brightly as her anger. Her emotions got the better of her. She went after the creature with her bare hands supported by magic.

The harpy barely lifted one claw and tossed her aside. Sunshine hit her head against a park bench and rolled through the scorched grass before she gathered her wits to attack again.

But found Aine blocking her way.

"You cannot win this battle," Aine crooned. "Forgive me. I know your pain, but we are leaving this place." She gently folded Sunshine into her arms and bore her away across the sea breezes that finally wafted them back to the detective agency.

Sunshine blinked. "Where are we? What are you doing?" She glared at Aine. "I can't believe you brought me back here. I had her. Another attack would've been the end. We may never find her again. It might have been our only shot to destroy her."

"For you," Aine agreed. "The harpy is not a werewolf or any other kind of enchanted creature you have ever met. She cannot be killed so easily. And she has already marked you forever."

Sunshine glanced into the mirror near Jane's desk. A large red scratch marred her smooth pink complexion. She put a hand to it, closing her eyes to summon a healing spell, and turned again to Aine.

"You don't get to make decisions like that for me. You don't know if my magic would have killed her. You barely gave me a chance, and now we've lost her."

"My apologies if my actions spared your life. I didn't realize you went there to die."

In anger, Sunshine threw a fire ball at Aine. The *beane‑sidhe* ignored it, stepping to the side.

"You're not a harpy," Sunshine said. "You can't avoid my magic forever."

Mr. Bad bellowed from his office. "In here now, if you please."

Sunshine gave Aine a scornful glance and then went toward the dark office.

"What happened?" Jane asked.

"It is a tale best told at another time," Aine replied before she joined Sunshine.

Neither woman took a seat before the massive desk. They kept their eyes on the shadowy figure behind it. Only the curtain at the window rippled as he faced them.

"You found the harpy," he said.

"Yes. Why didn't you tell me that's what killed John?" Sunshine demanded.

"Because you would have done exactly what you did tonight. You are impulsive, Miss Merryweather. You don't think before you act."

"Impulsive? You call killing the monster that killed John impulsive? Aine doesn't get to judge me—and neither do you. I'm going back out to find that thing and kill it. Neither one of you can stop me. If you want to sit here in your chair and let things happen to the people around you, that's your business. Stay out of mine."

In a flash of blinding silver light, Sunshine was gone.

"Surely you expected this, my lord." Aine wished she'd stopped the witch from leaving.

"I did indeed. I hoped her response would be tempered by your own. I expected too much in this emotionally charged situation."

"I shall confine her until something can be done about the harpy."

"No. She must be allowed to mature. Her heart will not be whole again until the creature is dead."

"Her heart will not be whole if the creature catches her," Aine reminded him. "Tell me, are there weapons here that could kill the harpy—part magic and part manmade? In my time, I know they existed, but in this day, I would not know where to begin looking for them."

"Alas. I fear the weapons needed are gone. If they have been hidden, I do not know where to find them."

"And you will not kill it?"

"No. I dare not. There is a reason I am here, Aine. I cannot reveal myself as yet."

She nodded. "You sentence more to die, perhaps the witch as well."

"What I do here is more important than the harpy.

Sunshine won't die. Not yet."

"Then I shall take my leave of you."

"Beware that you do not forget why you have come."

Chapter Eighteen

It was getting light by the time Aine reached the Chinese pagoda park where they'd found the harpy. All that remained was her prey. She went quickly to alert O'Neill once she discerned that all danger was past. The scent of the creature was gone.

O'Neill and Malto met at the beautiful crime scene with a large force of uniformed officers behind them. They searched the shadowed paths but found no clue of where the killer had gone. The park around them was well lit with the large red pagoda in the center of it. Lovely pools of water and plentiful koi leapt when they heard voices.

"The press is gonna eat this up," Malto told her partner as she stared at the assorted body parts that remained. "They're already calling this guy the Phantom Killer."

"Maybe someone will help us out by spotting him." O'Neill saw Aine waiting for him near a large oak tree and excused himself.

"Can't we go anywhere without her following?" Malto demanded. "Is she some kind of police groupie? Really, O'Neill? Maybe she's even the killer, the way she turns up everywhere."

He ignored her. He hadn't seen Aine when she'd awakened him in Elena's bed. But there was no going back to sleep after she'd made sure he'd seen the crime scene in his dreams.

"Thanks for the heads up, I think." He grimaced. "Next time, how about just telling me there's been a murder? I don't know if I'll ever get that image out of my mind. That's why they made cell phones, you know."

"I pray you don't see the creature feasting then, O'Neill," she retorted. "It is a terrible sight to behold, even for one such as I."

"Why didn't you stop her if you caught her at it?" He glanced around uneasily. "Where's Sunshine now?"

"Even now she hunts the creature. I alone cannot stop the harpy. Even with the witch's magic, we are not strong enough. The enchantment that created the harpy is older than I and from a time when gods walked the earth. I do not know how or if she will be killed."

"Good to know." He shook his head. "What about modern weapons—grenades, guns, missiles—any of that do anything to her?"

Aine thought about Mr. Bad's words regarding the harpy. "It may be possible. But I must find Sunshine before she is able to find the creature. Goodbye, O'Neill."

"Let me come with you. You and Sunshine might need help." He touched her hand as he spoke.

She immediately became the beautiful, young queen who had only been real in dreams since her death. Her tender gaze softened on his amazed features as he beheld her.

"Aine? Is that you?"

"Aye, O'Neill. It is me—at least part of me." She smiled, and with no thought for the consequences of her actions, she slowly put her pink lips to his and tasted the sweet wine of his mouth.

They kissed and clung, O'Neill's arms going around her pliable curves, no thought for the park full of police or the bloodthirsty harpy that might be nearby. She swayed, young and soft, smelling of flowers and spring air. He pulled her closer and drew in more of her sweetness, intoxicated by her.

"I must go."

He opened his eyes, and she was gone. He gulped hard as he heard Malto calling for him, wondering if he was losing his mind.

* * *

Aine found Sunshine on a rooftop just after daylight. There was no sign of the harpy. She was glad to see that the witch was unharmed but for the ugly gash on her face.

Sunshine was facing the Atlantic Ocean as she watched the sky lighten across the city. "This is a beautiful place, you know? I was born here. I've never thought of living anywhere else, even though I've traveled around the world."

"I never thought to go elsewhere myself." Aine sat beside her. "The hills of home are so green. Every day is like a miracle of color."

"We all have our weak spots. Yours is O'Neill. Mine is this thing with John, I guess." She shook her head. "It's not like I think I'll never love again. I know there will always be someone new—I'm elderly according to human standards. I'm going to live a long life. Most lovers age quickly. I won't be able to hold on to any one person."

Aine lifted her eyes to the sky above them. "'Tis true. Yet how glorious are those moments of love and passion in our lives. I have lived so long without feeling. Sometimes I almost forget what it was."

Sunshine stood beside her. "I'm sorry about those things I said to you. I thought if we could just find her, we could kill her, and I could move on. I realize now that it won't be that easy."

"And I am sorry I took you against your will. I did not want you to die." Aine faced her. "The creature can die. Mr. Bad and I have spoken of it. I believe he has the right notion of how it can be done, but the time must be precise. We shall have to attack her with magic, strength, and modern weapons. Only then can she be vanquished."

"I get that." Sunshine lightly touched the wound on her face. "I can't heal it—at least not yet."

"There is poison in her talons. Only your magic saved you from death. I have never known a harpy cut to heal. They fester where they slash and remain open wounds which—"

"Yeah. Please don't say anymore. I get the idea." Sunshine sighed. "I'm not giving up. There are stronger healing spells. Or I might have go to Wilmington and get some help from my family."

Aine nodded. "Perhaps your Aunt Molly's amulet. MacLir was known to heal in his time, as well as destroy."

The two women gazed over the rooftops around them. In the distance, huge ships were coming into harbor for repair and replenishing of their supplies. Birds cried as the lights of the city went dark in preparation for the coming day. Early risers were making their way to work and nightshift workers yawned as they started home.

"Looks like a whole new day. We survived the night. If you and Mr. Bad think we can kill this thing, I promise not to go off half-assed again. But now we have to find her and we know she's still hunting for those other shifters."

"Perhaps we should do some hunting ourselves," Aine said. "If we cannot search out the creature, let us find those she hunts and give them shelter from her rage."

Sunshine considered it. "Great idea! Thanks, Aine. Let's get off this roof. I need a shower and a change of clothes. Are you sure you can't change yours, except for the three forms you do by magic? The green dress and crown are kickass, but the black cloak and the rags—not so much. I have a little black dress that would really show off your legs. And we could go shopping for others."

"Why do you travel in the purple car when you can fly invisibly anywhere?" Aine asked.

"Because I like my convertible. And I like celebrating my humanity." Sunshine rose slowly into the air like the sun coming over the ocean. "I'm not just a good-looking witch with extraordinary magic, you know. I'm a gorgeous woman who enjoys being seen."

Sunshine became invisible for the trip back to the detective agency. Aine was never visible when she rode the air currents. They arrived at the same time in the outer office giving Jane such a fright that she dropped her cup of tea and scurried away in her mouse form.

"I'll be back in a few minutes," Sunshine said. "I'll feel better after I've had something to eat and drink. I think you'd feel better if you had something too."

Aine began to search for the mouse. "I appreciate the thought, but it is not necessary. The form you see me in as the tattered crone is my true form as my body falls to dust in my tomb."

"Really?" Sunshine kicked off her purple heels. "We'll have to visit sometime. Is it a national monument or something?"

"No. It is part of my penance that I lie alone within a mountain where people have forgotten me. Very few, if any, still know my name."

"Except on *Wikipedia*," Jane squeaked before she resumed her human form.

"*Wi-ki-ped-ia?*" Aine asked. "They know me in that land?"

"Going to shower now." Sunshine called the elevator. "Keep that page open when you find it, Jane. I want to see it too."

Leaving the two women to search for Aine's history, Sunshine went up to her room and showered. She felt better until she glanced into the steamy mirror. Aine was right. No healing spell she'd tried had eased the wound on her face. It wasn't painful, which was a blessing, but it was ugly and raw.

She tried a stronger spell on the scratch before she went to find a dress for the day. Only purple would do for the mood she was in. The dress had a shirt waist and full skirt with embroidered violets along the bodice and hem. Her purple pumps were filthy from running through the park and other endeavors of the night. She reached for a black pair but longed for the purple. A small spell made them look good as new. She put them on and went back to the bathroom mirror.

Her hair was full of nervous energy tinged with fear, which made it a shade darker, almost red. She studied her face again before ignoring the cut and adding lipstick. She wasn't going to let some bare-breasted harpy with poison claws ruin her day.

"And you just watch out," she warned the creature. "I'm going to find you again, and this time I'm going to kill you."

Was it her imagination, or had the cut on her face begun to burn?

Sunshine went back downstairs to look at the *Wikipedia* page and find something for breakfast. A painting of Aine, and a wonderful old tapestry that depicted her life, were on the computer screen.

"You were a warrior!" Sunshine clapped her on the back in her excitement at seeing Aine in silver armor on a white horse.

It was embarrassing for Aine to see her life spread out in this fashion. She'd always bemoaned her fate to be forgotten by the world, and yet this was far worse.

"Is there some way to remove it?" she asked Jane.

"No. It's part of Irish history—you're part of ancient history." Jane frowned at the dates listed on the page. "Were you really alive back then? And why isn't there a date of death listed?"

Aine turned away from the computer and walked into

Sunshine's office.

"I think she might be a little more sensitive about being dead than she realized." Sunshine hugged Jane and followed Aine. She closed the door behind her. "Sorry about that. Sometimes the internet is wonderful but sometimes not. Would you like to talk about it?"

"I would not." Aine left the window and sat in a chair by the desk. "How shall we lure the other shifters into a trap for the harpy?"

Sunshine went along with the abrupt change in conversation. "We'll have Jane find their addresses and bring them here for their own good."

"Here? There could be catastrophic damage to your home."

"It's the safest place I know. I can start working on new protection spells right away. Once we get the harpy here, we should be able to deal with her—one way or another."

"Please tell me you do not believe you can talk to this creature and win her over in your favor?"

"I don't see why not." Sunshine glanced at her email as she spoke. "People have feared many types of creatures, and yet now we know they mostly live among us without incident."

Aine shook her head. "It is your plan, but be prepared to use more than spells and good wishes to keep her from killing you. We should acquire modern weaponry as well if we hope to prevail."

Jane knocked at the door. "O'Neill is here. Do you want me to tell him that you're in a meeting?"

Sunshine heaved a heavy sigh. "You can't ask me that with him standing right behind you." She waved to O'Neill. "It's all right. Come on in. We were actually just talking about you."

O'Neill had showered and changed clothes too. Aine sniffed the artificial scents both he and Sunshine wore. It reminded her of how different—how *not* human—she was.

She turned her face away from him in shame as she remembered her moment of weakness when she'd felt something else about her charge. She couldn't let that happen again.

And yet she couldn't quite forget the firm pressure of his lips on hers.

"Would you like some coffee, O'Neill?" Jane asked sweetly as he walked into the room.

"Thanks, Jane," he said with a smile. "I could probably use another cup."

"I'd like another cup of tea," Sunshine said. She glanced at Aine but didn't bother her about it. "Did you learn anything from Marcus Fletcher's death?"

O'Neill took a seat. "Good morning, Aine."

When she didn't reply or even look at him, he moved on to the question Sunshine had asked. "Not really. Nothing new anyway. We know he was killed by the same method that killed the other men. We even found another feather. My assistant medical examiner says that the feather is artificial. He says it doesn't come from a real bird and has nothing to do with the case even though this is the second time we've found one."

"That doesn't surprise me." Sunshine took her cup of tea from Jane with a thank you. "People want to ignore things they fear or don't understand. Trust me. I've had a lifetime of experience with it."

"So what's on the agenda for today?" He thanked Jane for the coffee. "I figure I might as well shadow the two of you since you seem to be at the heart of it all."

He stared at Aine as he spoke, but she still gave no acknowledgement that he was there.

"Excuse me." Sunshine smiled. "I need more honey for my tea. I'll be right back."

As soon as she was gone—taking Jane with her—O'Neill put down his coffee.

"Are you all right?" he questioned Aine. "I thought

about you all night. It's difficult for me to understand any of this with it coming at me so quickly. I know you're here to warn me of my death and help me after I die. I even found a few other aspects to the *beane sidhe* on Google. I've been doing a lot more reading since I met you."

Aine shook her head. "The magic box is a curse."

"A lot of people think so."

"I am ready to answer any questions you might have. It is part of my service to your family to see that you are properly educated."

"I get that." He stood up and cornered her, managing to make her face him. "What about last night? I can't find anything about *beane sidhes* having romantic feelings toward the people they serve. Does that always happen?"

She immediately became the tattered crone, black eye sockets staring into his. "Do not mention it again, O'Neill."

He moved away from her quickly, shuddering despite himself. "I guess this is the harbinger of death mode you go into. What about the sweet, young woman in green? Where is she?"

"Leave it be, boy." Her coarse voice was filled with the terrors of the grave, shaking the room around them. "Do not mock me."

Sunshine had purposely left the two alone since they were obviously having difficulties. She hurried back when she realized those difficulties could involve wrecking her office.

"Plenty of honey now," she said nervously as she took her seat. "Shall we take a look at the board?" She snapped her fingers, and the clear board became visible.

O'Neill wasn't quite prepared for that. He was still stunned by Aine's warning. Confronting a magic suspect board was nearly his undoing. He rapidly sat down and clutched his coffee cup.

"Oh. Sorry. I've gotten so used to you being here." Sunshine patted his hand. "I forget that some of these things are new to you."

"Yeah." He dared a peek at Aine.

Sunshine laughed and got up to point out the faces on the board. "These are the last three shifters that we think are being targeted by the harpy."

He stopped writing in his notebook. "Shifters?"

"You know—all of them might be cat shifters of one kind or another. I think John mentioned that Tom Knox shifts into a lion, but don't quote me on that."

"And what did John Lancaster shift into?" O'Neill picked up on the pattern.

"John was a werewolf, like Marcus Fletcher. A shifter of sorts," Sunshine explained. "Except that he only became the wolf when the moon was full. Most shifters are like Jane and can change whenever they like."

O'Neill clutched his coffee cup again. "Jane? What does she shift into?"

"A mouse. Well, actually she's a mouse who shifts into a woman. Would you like to see?" Sunshine offered, ready to call her assistant.

"No. Not really." He cleared his throat. "Let's stay focused. What are you thinking about these…shifters?"

"We were thinking about bringing them here so the harpy has to come to us instead of her randomly picking them off on the street. Doesn't that sound like a good idea?"

Chapter Nineteen

"Maybe it would be better if Malto and I bring them in for questioning," O'Neill suggested. "That way we'll have the entire police department backing us."

"Except for one small detail," Sunshine said. "The harpy can't be killed by normal weapons, nor can she be killed with magic alone. We're going to have to combine our strengths if we want to get rid of her. That would be better done here, without Malto and the rest of the police department."

She wanted to slap Aine. The *beane sidhe* was sitting there like a lump in her black gown and cape. At least she wasn't going all dead crone on them, but this was her idea too. She was supposed to help with it. What was wrong with her anyway? She'd caught a little of their conversation but not enough to know what was going on, though she had her suspicions.

"I suppose that makes sense," he agreed. "I'd rather Malto not know about all this. I don't think she'd take it well."

What can I do to help?"

"What's the biggest gun you can lay your hands on?"

He thought it over. "Probably an assault rifle. A friend of mine has a grenade launcher, but I don't think you'd want to use that here."

Sunshine's blue eyes got wide. "No. I definitely wouldn't want to use a grenade launcher here. But thanks for asking. I guess an assault rifle will have to do. The first thing is to find the three shifters. Once we get them all under one roof then we can proceed with our plan for the harpy."

"Sounds like you've got it all figured out." O'Neill nodded. "I could bring in one or two of the shifters."

"That might be dangerous for you." Sunshine didn't want to discourage his participation, but an angry shifter could kill him which would fulfill Aine's death prophecy and set off a chain reaction that none of them wanted. "Why don't you let us handle that? You bring the rifle when I tell you. Is that okay?"

"Why don't you let me come with you?" he proposed. "That way I don't feel like a woman in a dress with violets on it is doing my job. I promise to stay back away from claws and teeth, unless you need me."

Sunshine looked at Aine for input. How would she feel about endangering O'Neill's life? "Does that work for you?"

"You know my feelings on the subject." Aine didn't look up, her words muttered from beneath her hood. "O'Neill's life must be safeguarded."

"Wait a minute," he protested. "This is part of my job. We talked about this. There's some danger to being a police detective. It goes with the territory."

"If 'twould be simpler for you," Aine offered, "I could lock ye in a cellar somewhere."

O'Neill got to his feet, ready to confront her.

Sunshine got between them. "Why don't we plan on you helping us? Get the rifle you need and come back. We'll wait for you. Aine and I will talk this over while you're gone."

"I'm not hiding out somewhere because my *beane sidhe* doesn't want me to die." He glared at Aine. "I'm doing this. You might as well get used to it."

Aine opened her mouth, and Sunshine put her hand over it. "All right. See you later."

"How dare you touch me in such a way?" Aine rose to her feet and glared at her after O'Neill had left them.

"You didn't give me much choice. You sit there not talking, not helping at all, and just bother to open your mouth to scare O'Neill and shake the building. You know I'm not impressed by that." Sunshine tossed her hair. "Well, I was the first time, but I've seen it now. So sit down and tell me what's really wrong."

Sunshine wasn't sure if Aine would comply. She certainly couldn't make her do it. She was glad when Aine finally sat back down.

"I kissed O'Neill."

"What? No. Wait. I need more tea, and Jane needs to be in here. You don't want to repeat the story, do you?"

Aine hung her head and didn't speak until the other women were in the office. "I kissed O'Neill."

Jane laughed and then put her hand to her lips. "Where?"

"At the park last night, with the stench of dead wolf and harpy in the air. It was a disgrace, but I could not entirely control it."

"But *where* did you kiss him?" Jane continued. "Cheek? Forehead? Lips?"

With a heavy sigh Aine shook her head. "His lips. I kissed his lips, damn you!"

"But how did it happen?" Sunshine kept pouring honey into her tea until it was too sweet, but she gulped it down anyway. "Were you two talking about something romantic, even though you were close to the wolf kill? Or were you—?"

"Do the pair of you have nothing better to do than to hear my story?" Aine's voice was anguished. "I made a mistake. I don't know what came over me."

"*Let me tell you 'bout this thing called love,*" Jane started singing in a sweet, high-pitched voice.

"Silence mouse!"

Jane stopped singing but glanced across the room at Sunshine.

"No. We want to hear it all, Aine," Sunshine said. "You started it. Now you have to finish. It'll be good for you."

"Why did you kiss him?" Jane asked as she stuffed uncooked popcorn into her mouth from her pockets.

"I do not know," Aine admitted. "It simply happened."

"He touched you, didn't he?" Sunshine asked with a knowing expression on her face. "You two have a thing. Maybe you don't like it, but there it is."

"They have a thing," Jane whispered as she nodded.

"How can I guide him and protect him with this between us?" Aine demanded. "It's not possible. I must right this wrong. Perhaps if I ignore him and frighten him, our relationship will become more normal."

"Nah," Jane said. "I watch soap operas every day. The more you ignore him, the more he's gonna want you. That's the way it is. I'm not sure about scaring him."

"She's right. And it works for men being frightened of you too. Once, before I met John, there was this shifter—" Sunshine put aside her tepid tea and looked up at them. "No. We don't need to talk about that."

"Sunshine!" Jane pleaded.

"We have bigger problems right now." She backed out of the corner she'd put herself in. "We have to find those three shifters, hopefully still alive, and get them in here."

"I already know where they live," Jane said. "I pulled up neighborhood maps for each of them. I can send those to your phone. That should help you find them."

"Great." Sunshine checked the first map. "All we have to do is convince them to come with us because their lives are in danger. And you're right, Aine. If we could keep O'Neill out of this part, it would be good. But we need him for the rifle part. I don't know about you, but I've never fired any kind of weapon."

"There were no such things in my day, though I have observed their use." The *beane sidhe* raised herself to her full height. "I am quite skilled with other weapons, including the bow and the javelin."

"Good," Sunshine said. "I didn't know a javelin was a weapon. I thought it was more a sports thing, but we're on the same page. We need our magic and O'Neill's rifle to subdue the harpy."

"What are you going to do with her once she's subdued?" Jane asked.

"Good question, my dear Watson." Sunshine smiled at her assistant. Both women looked blankly at her, with no idea what she was talking about. "Forget it. I don't know right now. Let's get the shifters in here first, and then we'll handle the rest."

Aine and Sunshine left to find the first shifter on the map that Jane had sent. He was only a few blocks from the detective agency. Sunshine decided not to drive since she was worried about having to force the shifter to accompany them. He might damage the upholstery in her convertible.

"Surely we do not have to walk these crowded streets," Aine said as they started down the sidewalk. Several people walked into her as she stalked down the concrete.

"It's a beautiful day," Sunshine said. "Why not walk? The exercise is good for you."

Aine lifted her brows at that suggestion.

"It's good for me," Sunshine decided. "You can fly over there with the wind, if you like. I enjoy an occasional stroll."

Her pronouncement was met with silence, but Aine continued to walk beside her. She never moved to the side for any pedestrians. If they walked into her and asking her pardon, glancing up into her face changed their minds.

"Does the harpy's scratch pain you?"

Sunshine moved her hand away from the mark. "Only a little. It didn't hurt at all last night. This morning it started."

"Fortunate that you are powerful or you would most certainly lie dead. Most do not survive the harpy's attack."

"As soon as this is over I'll head down to visit my family and they'll know what to do. I've tried every healing spell I know. It still looks disgusting. I'm glad I'm not dating. Otherwise I'd have to go through the whole invisibility spell to keep him from seeing it."

"I have told you that you are fortunate to be alive, and all you can consider is your beauty?" Aine shook her head in disgust. "You are most vain."

"Let's talk about that." Sunshine nudged her with an elbow. "When you were about to kiss O'Neill, did you turn into the ratty, old crone, or did you become the pretty, young queen?"

"It did not happen that way." Aine growled at a man who walked into her. He quickly got out of her way. "He touched me, and I became my youthful self. Then I kissed him."

"Oh. Forgive me, Your Majesty." Sunshine bowed to her. "I didn't mean to mess with your timeline."

"You mock me."

"Yes. I do. But only because you said I was vain. And here we are. See how a little mocking helps the time go by faster? Let's talk to the shifter."

Tom Knox was hiding in his apartment. After the death of two of his friends and the men at *Tattoo Hell*, he was smart in considering that he could be next. He remembered Sunshine's name and let her come upstairs, glancing around the hall as he opened his door to her.

Tom was every inch a tawny lion shifter. He had a huge mane of blond hair and brown eyes that could melt snow. His body rippled when he moved wearing thin, cropped shirt and shorts that barely covered him. He was taller and broader than Aine, with large feet and hands.

Sunshine took a moment to gawk—cat shifters were always so beautiful. She was barely able to keep herself from touching him.

But he was also terrified.

"I had no idea any of this was coming at me," he said after double bolting his door behind them. "I mean, I knew something was wrong when John was killed. I didn't know what it was until the tattoo dudes were killed too. I still don't understand it."

"Do you have any idea why the harpy wants to kill you?" Sunshine asked him. "Or some idea who she serves?"

"No! I don't know. I can't think of anything we did to deserve this. John was a good guy. So was Marcus. Amos too. We hung out together, which some people think is wrong because like should stay with like, but murder us for it? Come on. This is the twenty-ish century."

"Twenty-first century," Sunshine corrected. Okay. He wasn't very bright, but he was gorgeous.

She wished she could get a grasp on who was sending the harpy. Maybe it was someone who hated handsome shifters. Maybe it was, as Tom suggested, someone who thought the shifters were too friendly with the wolves. She'd heard some nonsense like it before, but not in a long time.

Was there some offense done by the group of shifters that seemed slight to them but a big deal to someone else? It could be anything—women, territory, or money.

Without finding the harpy first to locate the person who was using her to exact revenge, they might never know. That scared Sunshine. She didn't want to get caught up in a war between magical creatures. And yet it seemed that she already was.

"Come with us," she encouraged Tom. "We can keep you safe until we figure it out."

"And we can use you to lure the harpy to her death," Aine added.

Tom might have considered Sunshine's more pleasant sounding offer but not with Aine's addition. "I'm not sticking out my neck so you can figure what's going on. I'll just wait here until it's over. Thanks anyway."

Aine faced him fearlessly. "You are vital to our plan. Therefore you will accompany us back to the agency. I do not care if you are willing."

He growled loudly at her, showing his enlarged teeth as he partially changed enough to warn her. "I'm not going anywhere with you, lady. You both better leave now. You don't want to see me when I'm angry."

"Trust me." Sunshine stepped between them. "You don't want to see her when she's angry. And she's already dead, so threatening her doesn't mean anything. Come along peacefully. There's a good lion. We'll send out for pizza. We know how to take care of you."

Tom didn't seem ready to back down from the challenge. He growled again and exposed his razor sharp claws. "I'm not going anywhere." His voice ended in a deep growl.

Aine immediately changed to the crone. Her voice drove him to his knees, hands clapped over his ears as he begged her to stop.

"Okay. Okay." He glanced up at her terrifying face. "What the hell are you anyway?"

"I am the O'Neill *beane sidhe*," she declared. "You will come with us as we require, or I shall drag you to the underworld."

"All right. I get it." Tom got to his feet—minus claws and fangs. "Let's go, but be careful. That harpy thing took Amos right out on the street and shredded him in front of everyone."

"Not to worry." Sunshine grasped his hand. "We move with the breeze, shifter. Hold on."

They arrived back at the agency in an instant. Sunshine made sure Tom was comfortable with TV, video games, and plenty of snacks. Jane refused to go near with the scent of cat on him. She hid in Sunshine's office, staring at the computer.

"One down," Sunshine told Aine. "Two to go. Although it occurs to me that we only need one of them to attract the harpy. Maybe we should let the other two stay where they are."

"We have no way of knowing which of the three she will come for first," Aine reminded her. "If she kills the other two, your conscience will bother you."

"What about your conscience?" Sunshine demanded.

"I have none. I had very little when I was alive. Dead, nothing I do bothers me if it means I may achieve my ends."

"And it's just not right," Jane added. "If you can save them, you should. Even if they are cats."

"Yeah. I know. I was just joking." Sunshine looked at her phone for the second address. "I guess this one we'll get in the car. It's a good day for a drive."

"What about the destruction of your car?" Aine questioned.

"This one was probably the worst. I'm sure none of them will want to stay where they are when we offer them shelter—especially the way you do it." She checked her hair, which had rearranged itself despite the wound on her face. "By the way, can you really drag someone to the underworld if you want to? Is that a real thing? Because while that is an awesome threat, it would be a better reality."

"Come along." The expression on Aine's face approached that of a smile. "It's best you don't know all I am capable of."

"That sounds like a challenge." Sunshine grinned. "Women with hair like mine never back down from a challenge."

"Are you gonna call for pizza for reals?" Tom's voice whined into the smaller office. "I'm getting real hungry here."

"Time for us to go," Sunshine recommended. "Call for

pizza delivery, Jane. Make sure there is plenty of it."

"You got it." Jane nibbled on her nails as she picked up the phone.

"Let's find Ms. Godfrey," Sunshine said to Aine. "Be ready with that dragging-someone-to-
hell line."

Aine insisted that the underworld was not the hell of Christian mythology as they drove to pick up Irene Godfrey.

Sunshine argued that it didn't matter—calling it hell sounded more dramatic and people threatened with it would be more afraid. "Not to mention that the underworld sounds more like a club."

"I believe I am sufficiently fearful enough to accomplish our goals."

"It never hurts to be scarier. You just never know what someone's tolerance for being scared is. Some people are terrified of spiders. Some people probably aren't afraid of you, though I can't imagine why."

"I understand. I shall endeavor to be as frightening as I am able. I don't believe the god of the underworld will care if I misname his home for a good purpose."

"God of the underworld?" Sunshine laughed at that. "Really? Is there such a thing?"

"You more than most should know the answer to that question."

"You mean because I'm a witch and know lots of secret stuff? I've just never heard of the god of the underworld— unless you mean that old myth of Satan in Hell. Or are you talking about older times? Greek or Roman? Maybe Egyptian? What were their names? Did you know any of them?"

Sunshine threw out the questions as she guided the convertible through traffic on Princess Anne Boulevard in the heart of the city. She didn't see the body falling from the blue sky above her until it was too late. She swerved sharply to the right, hitting another vehicle. But the bloody corpse still

came down squarely on the hood of her car.
"You've gotta be kidding me!"

Tom was every inch a tawny lion shifter.

Chapter Twenty

Irene Godfrey was very dead. What the harpy didn't do to her, the drop from the sky did.

The police came shortly after. Sunshine was miserable about her car and that they'd lost another of the shifters to the harpy.

"You're in the middle of the street, Miss Merryweather," the uniformed officer told her. "There's no way somebody jumped off a building and fell on your car."

"Ask anybody," she argued. "The woman fell on my car. I didn't hit her."

But when she looked around her at the other drivers and looky-loos who'd had to stop for her, they were all shaking their heads. Everyone thought she'd hit Irene Godfrey and the body had flown up and bounced back on her car.

"Okay. Let's settle this somewhere else so we can get this moved off the street," the cop decided. He glanced into the ruined convertible. "What about you, lady? Are you getting out or what?"

An older, green Honda pulled up out of the tangled traffic mess. It was O'Neill and Malto. They told Sunshine to wait by her car while they spoke with the officer.

"The law-givers will learn the truth soon enough now that O'Neill is here," Aine said. "It was a ridiculous assumption on their part that you would hit anything with this much beloved car of yours."

"And in the meantime—while we're sitting here—the harpy is going after Lloyd." Sunshine stamped her foot. "She's got us at every turn. If we don't come up with something to handle her, she'll keep killing."

O'Neill and Malto were finished talking with the police officers who'd begun taking care of the traffic, getting it moving around the convertible and making room for the ambulance that had swerved into their lane.

"Anybody hurt?" He flicked a glance at Aine. "We're taking over this case as part of our ongoing investigation."

"I'm fine," Sunshine said. "Thank you for coming. We've got Tom Knox back at the office, but we couldn't get to Irene before this happened."

"What about her?" Malto pointed to Aine. "I've never seen anyone sit in a car after an accident if there wasn't anything wrong with them."

"She's okay too," Sunshine assured her. "Just stunned. It happened so quickly."

"I brought Malto up to speed on the case," O'Neill told her. "She knows that you and Aine are witches and that you're having a street war with some other, bad witches."

"Yeah," Malto agreed. "But unless the bad witches ride broomsticks and dropped this woman on the car, no way she jumped this far from a building. Did blondie get rid of the rival witch or what?"

"I explained that you might see some unusual things," he said. "There are a lot of drugs involved."

"Shouldn't we call DEA then?" Malto asked. "Hey! I'm

not on drugs!"

"Do we want credit for the collar, or do we want them to have it?" he asked her. "We can read them in once we know we've got the killers. They can take care of the drugs at that point."

"Yeah. Okay. Here comes the tow truck for the car." Malto glanced at Sunshine. "We're gonna have to impound it as part of the case. Sorry. You two girls need a ride? We can call you a taxi."

But O'Neill told her he'd be taking Sunshine and Aine back to the detective agency. Malto agreed to wait for the morgue pickup for Irene Godfrey.

Sunshine sat in the front seat of the green Honda as he drove to the office. "We appreciate your help with this."

He glanced in the rearview mirror at Aine, who hadn't spoken a word. "Are you sure she's okay?"

"She's fine. Have you had a chance to find Lloyd? The harpy has to be after him."

"He's not at the pizza place where he works and he's not at home. I've got people out looking for him, but I think he's hiding from everyone. Not that I blame him."

"He won't be able to hide from her," Sunshine said. "So you told your partner this was some crazy witch war?"

"What else could I tell her? She wouldn't leave the office this morning until I explained what was going on. I had to tell her something. She doesn't believe you're a real witch, if that's what you're worried about—and I didn't mention the part about a *beane sidhe*. But she gets the whole thing on being crazy."

"I guess we do what we have to do." Sunshine glanced out the window. "You can let us out in front of the building. We'll wait to hear from you about finding Lloyd. Thank you for getting us out of that mess."

O'Neill pulled in front of the older, red brick building. "Sure. I'm glad I could get there so quickly. Staying here would be the best thing you could do right now."

Sunshine put her hand on his and breathed into his face. "I think you might be the best person to stay here. Why don't you take a little nap, and we'll be back in a while when we're finished borrowing your car."

He slumped over the steering wheel, sound asleep.

"What have you done?" Aine demanded.

"Relax. I only want to borrow his car and get him out of harm's way. I know you don't want him to get hurt. This way is best."

"You are deceptive." Aine checked him but he was well. "I shall take him inside. As you say, it is for the best."

She lifted O'Neill as though he were a child and took him in. She pulled him close to her chest, his head resting against her. He was going to be angry when he woke, but he would be safe. She would have done this herself if the witch hadn't thought of it.

Aine had never experienced such tender feelings for a charge before. She was becoming impossibly foolhardy in her dotage. She shouldn't be worried about his death—it would finally free her. And yet she fought to protect him.

"One of us should stay here." Sunshine followed her. "If we can't find Lloyd or she kills him first, she'll come here next."

"What about Mr. Bad?" Aine carefully placed O'Neill on the sofa. "Surely he would assist us."

"He helps us with ideas. He isn't a fighter," Sunshine explained. "I know you can handle it if she shows up here."

Aine watched Sunshine leave in O'Neill's car. For whatever reason, Mr. Bad had chosen to keep his identity hidden. Perhaps as with many ancient creatures, he feared what this world might do to him. It was not her place to question his decision. She didn't fear the harpy, although she knew it was probably not possible for her to destroy it by herself. She could at the very least keep it from harming Tom Knox.

"Does the magic box have any notion of why these

specific creatures have been targeted?" Aine asked as she stepped into Sunshine's office.

Jane nearly jumped out of her chair. "I'm sorry. I didn't know you were here. Where's Sunshine?"

"She has gone to get the last shifter, if the harpy has not already taken his life." Aine explained about how they'd located Irene Godfrey. "The harpy does not hunt for sport. Someone has a reason for her to kill these people."

"I've looked around, but without knowing who's controlling her, I don't have any idea how to figure why she's doing it. Maybe whoever it is hates shifters."

"And only these shifters and the men at the tattoo shop have been found dead in such a manner?"

"I've thought of all the combinations I could to find another death like these—I've even hacked into the police database. There's nothing." Jane's tone was apologetic.

"Thank you. Do not fret," Aine said. "Sunshine says you are brilliant with this box. High praise indeed."

"Thanks." Jane blushed and smiled. "I wish I could do more. It came so easily to me, once I became human."

Aine went back into the outer office. Tom Knox was sleeping on a thick rug. O'Neill was sleeping on the sofa. She envied them their ability to shut out the world. Her body in the tomb slept, after a fashion, but she was here and never closed her eyes.

She looked deeply into O'Neill's face, seeing generations before him written into the essence of this man. She wished she could simply watch and wait until he was gone. Lying down in her tomb had been all she'd wished for during many years of her penance. Now she wanted O'Neill to marry and have a family. She wasn't sure what had changed—perhaps waking alone in Castle O'Neill.

After a few moments she found herself outside Mr. Bad's office door. She didn't have to knock to gain entrance. The door swung wide, inviting her into the darkness.

"You have questions," he said in his rasping voice.

"I do not seek to pry."

"Yet you don't understand why I keep myself from the world you've experienced."

"Though you have chosen to remain here, the witch tells me you will not take part in a battle against the harpy."

The chair he sat in made its usual creaking sound. "I can't take part in the events of today. I am forbidden by the others, even though I have been exiled from my home. I sit each day here in the darkness, waiting for the call to escape this place."

"And yet I sense you have feelings for the witch. You would not have stayed if you did not."

"Don't seek to put motive or words to my actions, Aine. They are beyond the understanding of even those such as you."

His voice sounded weary and bored. Aine could also sense an underlying frustration that was smoldering beneath his tone.

"I meant no disrespect, my lord. But I leave you to your thoughts with a word of caution."

He laughed. "You seek to warn me? Of what?"

"Even those of us who are mortal know that discontent can lead to mistakes. Beware of it."

"Thank you for your concern. How fares your O'Neill?"

"He is here under my protection, as is one of the shapeshifters that is hunted by the harpy."

"Here?" he thundered. "In my place of refuge?"

"Part of Sunshine Merryweather's plan to save the shifters and kill the harpy." Aine inclined her head respectfully with a smile on her face that she was glad he couldn't see. "Even when we think there are no surprises, matters happen that amaze us. Good day."

Jane was outside the office door, hopping from one foot to another as she waited for Aine to emerge from Mr. Bad's dark domain. "I can't believe it. It was just there, and I didn't notice it before, but I found it. Another death, I mean. At least I think I found it. I'm not completely sure, but it might be something. I need some seeds."

Aine watched as Jane rushed to the kitchen and returned with her mouth bulging with seeds.

"You're human now," Aine acknowledged. "Surely a cup or a bowl would be put to better use."

Jane kept running toward Sunshine's office. She spit the seeds on the desk and grinned at Aine with dozens of them still stuck in her teeth. "The best way to carry things. Sit down. Let me show you what I found."

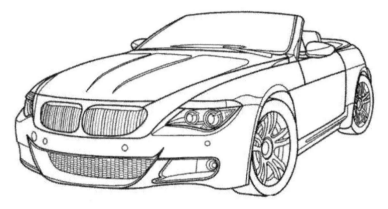

"The woman fell on my car. I didn't hit her."

Chapter Twenty-one

Aine sat in a chair close to Jane and the computer. She peered at the screen, even though it made her feel as though her eyes were crossed.

"See here—I was looking in Norfolk for deaths where people had been ripped apart." Jane glanced at her nervously. "You know what I mean."

"Continue."

"Well, there weren't any here, but there were two similar deaths in Richmond and one in Washington, DC."

"And were these the deaths of shifters?"

"I really don't know. I can't access that information because mostly the human world doesn't believe in shapeshifters—except in movies and books. It seems they enjoy reading about them, but they don't believe they're real."

"Odd. What has happened to mankind? Have they no belief in otherworldly creatures?"

"No. Not really. They believe in science and technology. Most humans think magic is dead."

Aine nodded. "I see. But you think these other three deaths relate to the ones here."

"Maybe. I can't be absolutely sure because we don't have a database of magic and enchanted creatures. It would be nice if we did."

"What about *Wikipedia*? I was dismayed to see myself there, but perhaps there is such a thing for shapeshifters."

"No," Jane replied. "*Wikipedia* probably has a general page for shifters, but a shifter would have to be famous or historical, like you, to have his own page."

"Did these murder victims have anything else in common?"

Jane glanced through the obituaries for the three victims that she'd found. "Well, two of them lived in Richmond, like I said. It was a man and a woman. They were married, in their fifties. Had children. Wait! They both worked for the State of Virginia. They both worked in the same office, which was where their bodies were found. Oh! It was the state office for grants, specifically artistic grants."

"I comprehend some of what you say. Are these grants from the king of artists?" Aine watched the images of where the two people were found fly by on the screen with the obituaries and put a hand to her head. They were quite dizzying.

"Not a king or a queen. But our government gives money to artists. The place where these two were killed funnels that money into the state."

"What about the dead one in the other land you mentioned?" Aine asked, not recalling what Jane had said. She had never heard of such a place.

"Washington," Jane repeated for her. "Let's take a look." She zoomed to the information she'd pulled up for that victim. "Guess what? That woman was in her forties, married with children, and worked for the National Arts Foundation. In other words, the place where the grant money came from in the first place."

"That was a great nap." Tom looked around the office as he smacked his lips and stretched. "I'm getting kind of hungry again. Got any pizza left?"

Jane shrieked and immediately became a small mouse in Sunshine's chair.

Frustrated as they were about to unfold some truth that could help them, Aine got to her feet. "Be gone, lazy bumpkin. There will be food a 'plenty when we finish our task. Do not enter here again or face my wrath."

"Okay. The witch said there would be enough to eat. I'm not trying to cause any trouble. A man could starve to death out here." Tom turned and went back to the outer office.

Aine closed the door behind him. "It is safe, little one. He will not bother us again."

Jane resumed her human form but anxiously stared at the door. "I should order more pizza. I'm sure O'Neill will be hungry when he wakes up too. And there's Lloyd. Sunshine might even want to eat."

She picked up the phone and ordered a dozen pizzas, adding the cost of them to the Purple Door Detective Agency's tab with the local pizzeria.

When that was done, and Jane seemed less upset by the shifter, Aine coaxed her into going back to the magic box for more information.

"What does all that mean?" she asked.

"I'm not completely sure," Jane admitted. "But it seems to me that three people in two other places who basically do the same job being ripped apart means something. We'll have to show it to Sunshine when she gets back. She'll know what it means."

Aine was angry that the words meant so little to her. She could understand much of the new language when she listened to speech carefully, but reading it was difficult. She was sure Jane was right, however. Sunshine would know what to make of it.

The front doorbell rang a few minutes later. Jane went to answer it, grateful and slightly less afraid, when Aine said she would accompany her. It seemed unlikely that the harpy would use this conventional means of breaching the building, but Aine wanted to make certain everyone was safe.

The pizza delivery man looked up at the tall woman dressed in black, and his mouth dropped. Jane took one of the boxes from him. Aine took the others.

"Uh...tip?" He held out his hand.

Aine looked at his delicate pink member and spit into it. "Thus I seal our transfer."

Horrified, the young man ran back to his car that had a pizza on top. Aine closed the door and locked it behind him with what seemed to be a delicate piece of metal to ban those who would enter without permission. Where was the wooden slab to bar the door?

"Pizza!" Tom jumped up from his place in front of the TV.

Jane lost control, reverting to her real self, and was covered by a large box holding a hot pepperoni pizza.

O'Neill sat up abruptly during the chaos and looked around himself. "What the hell is going on?"

Aine grabbed the pizza box and freed Jane before she flung   the   box   at   the   shifter. She set the other boxes on the table near the kitchen as the mouse skittered into the other room.

"Are you hungry, O'Neill?" She shook one of the boxes. "The smell isn't horrible, but the food seems hard and dry. Do you require other sustenance?"

"I don't require any sustenance," he said. "But some answers would be nice."

They all heard a key scrape in the door that Aine had just locked. She stood ready, facing it while O'Neill pulled his service revolver. Tom ran to hide in the kitchen.

Sunshine breezed through the door with Lloyd Samson right behind her. "Well. It looks like the party is ready to get started. I hope there's plenty of pizza."

Lloyd and Tom swapped tales of close calls that they'd been fortunate to survive as they bonded over pepperoni. O'Neill ended up taking a slice from Jane, despite his anger. Sunshine took two slices of cheese pizza and went into her office.

She was quickly joined by O'Neill, Jane, and Aine. Sunshine explained how she'd done a location spell and found Lloyd hiding in the sewer. She'd insisted on him cleaning up before they came back to the agency.

"There was no sign of the harpy this time," she said. "I'm sure she's still looking for the other two shifters. Every time I hear a swishing sound, I cringe. I'm not crazy about the idea of getting a harpy tangled in my hair."

"What about me?" O'Neill demanded. "You can't just go around putting spells on people—especially police detectives. And what was the point?"

Sunshine patted his hand. "We just want you to be safe. It's important to us."

He glanced at Aine. "You give me some witch's word that it won't happen again, or I'm walking out of here and spending the rest of my day on the street taking pot shots at anything that flies."

Aine's sharp intake of breath was noticeable in the quiet room when he was done speaking.

"There's no reason to be hostile," Sunshine said. "We were only doing what we thought was best for you. You are human, after all, with no magic to protect yourself."

He nodded at the wound on her face. "It doesn't look like magic helped you all that much."

"It would've killed you, detective," she said. "Aine is the only one of us who could survive a full-on harpy attack. But between us, we might have a chance against her. She's going to come here for Tom and Lloyd. Let's not bicker. We need to be united against her."

O'Neill studied her pretty face. "Don't use magic against me again. I'll go along with the team up. I'll keep your asses out of jail. But not unless I have your word that it won't happen again."

"You have my word, O'Neill." Aine's voice was quiet but certain. "She will never use magic against you again—or she will answer to me. I don't believe the witch wants that."

Sunshine calmly blotted her lips with a napkin to be certain there was no pizza left on them. "All right. You have my word that I won't use magic for or against you again, O'Neill."

Jane laughed timidly. "You should spit in his hand now. That's what Aine did when the pizza delivery guy asked for a tip."

O'Neill grinned. Sunshine shook her head.

"Your customs are strange to me," Aine said by way of explanation. "If that was not the proper response to ending our association, tell me, and I shall learn from the experience."

None of them said anything in answer to her query. Jane gathered the plates and napkins together.

"What do we do now?" O'Neill asked.

"We wait." Sunshine kicked off her pumps. "The harpy has been methodical about killing the shifters. I don't think it will take long for her to pick up their scent."

"I'm going to get my assault rifles."

"I shall accompany you," Aine said.

"I found something on the computer that you should see," Jane told Sunshine. "Aine thought it might be important too. I'm not sure."

"Let's take a look at it." Sunshine turned on her monitor.

Aine went outside before she would allow O'Neill through the door. She scanned the deep blue skies above them and sniffed the air. There seemed to be no sign of the harpy. She gestured to him that he could safely go to his car.

"You two are more worried about me than my own mother," he grumbled, taking out his car keys as he approached the green car. "I'm a grown man—a trained police detective with years of experience—I can take care of myself."

Aine kept her green eyes on the sky. "Hurry."

"From what I've read, you should be eager for me to die. You've already shrieked once for my death. I guess you're not that worried or you'd be screaming right now."

"I have never been eager for the death of an O'Neill,"

she assured him. "And the death song comes to me when it will. I do not sense your impending destruction at this moment, but we are all in the harpy's sights. Caution seems prudent."

He opened the trunk and took out three assault rifles with extra rounds. "But since I'm the last of my family line, you'd be free, right? You wouldn't have to stick around anymore. You could finally go to the underworld."

"Do not think of it so," she counselled. "Your time will come and I will be there for you."

She'd been scouting around them, watching for the harpy, ignoring what he was doing.

Before he removed the guns from the trunk, he reached out and grasped her hand. Aine immediately transformed into the younger version of herself. The sunlight glinted in the bright red strands of her hair. Her complexion was milk-smooth with hints of pink in her lips and cheeks. Her soft eyes were lined with thick, dark lashes.

"Who will be there to sing your death song and guide you to the underworld?" he asked in a low tone as he stared into her beautiful face.

"You understand little about me, O'Neill," she replied in a voice as sweet as summer. "This form was once me but no longer. I am *beane Sidhe*." She moved her hand from his and became the ragged crone. "This is my true form now as my body rots in my tomb. There will be no death song for me, and I do not hope for the peace of the underworld. Get your weapons. We should not tarry out here for long."

But O'Neill seemed to know the heart of her and didn't hesitate to call it back, despite that she was his protector. It frightened Aine and made her furious at the same time. She had nothing to threaten him with and could only stay away from him to keep it from happening again.

"I've got the guns," he said finally as he slammed the trunk closed. "Let's go."

There was no attack from the harpy. It could be that she

was only interested in them as targets if they had one of the shifters she sought. If so, Sunshine's current plan would work admirably.

Once they were back inside and the guns were stowed in a closet, O'Neill turned to Aine. "I'm sorry. You're right—I don't understand what you're all about. But I'd like to. I won't touch you again. I promise. I'd still appreciate it if you don't give up on me."

His statement was greeted with a disgusted huffing sound, and Aine walked away from him. What ploy was this? She had lost her touch when it came to dealing with O'Neill men. Or perhaps he wasn't sufficiently frightened of her. Their meeting was different, and their circumstances—working together—was unusual.

"I guess we're ready for her," Sunshine said brightly. She took a good look at the two of them, facing each other with bewildered and angry expressions, and knew what was wrong. "We just have to wait now. I think Jane is right about those other deaths being part of the whole thing. Why don't you go take a look at the computer, O'Neill?"

He grunted and left them with a last look at Aine.

She relaxed and resumed her middle-aged woman in black form. "Thank ye."

"What's wrong with you?" Sunshine took her into the kitchen for privacy. "He's gorgeous, and you own him. Why the shroud and black eyes?"

"I do not own O'Neill. If the truth be told, it would be closer to he owning me. But it is difficult to understand the relationship between the *beane sidhe* and her charge."

"Save me the speeches," Sunshine hissed. "There's something going on between you—I can feel the magic. Why not let it happen?"

"You are daft. There is nothing that shouldn't be there, unless it is that O'Neill is lacking the necessary fear of death he should experience when he sees me. Instead he insists on dragging out my younger form. I do not understand."

"You were hot." Sunshine winked as she made a cup of tea. "Of course he'd rather deal with you that way. The crone is kind of scary. This form in black is safe, but what young man wants to be safe?"

Aine thought about her words as they joined Jane and O'Neill in Sunshine's office. Lloyd and Tom were watching cartoons in the outer office. There was the edge of calm before the storm in the building.

O'Neill agreed that the deaths seemed too similar to be dismissed. "But who were her targets? Three people working for the grants end of the arts endowment. I don't get why anyone would be willing to kill for a grant."

"There was a large grant involved," Jane said. "It was over one hundred thousand dollars, not to mention several premier gallery showings for the artist ending at a gala presentation at the National Arts Museum in Washington."

"Hold on a sec." O'Neill looked at the screen again. "Jane, can you pull up the name of the winner? I suddenly have a bad feeling about this."

Jane did as he asked. The images changed, and the face of the winner was displayed on the monitor.

He ran his hand through his hair and left Sunshine's office without a word.

"Did he see a ghost?" Sunshine asked as she sat in the chair beside Jane. "The winner is Elena Spiros. Oh. My. God."

Aine stared at the face on the screen. "O'Neill's lover guides the harpy."

Jane grabbed a few seeds. "Yikes."

He opened the trunk and took out the assault rifles with extra rounds.

Chapter Twenty-two

"What?" Sunshine reached over and added something to the search on the computer. "Are you sure?"

"I am certain," Aine said. "I was with them as they made love."

The two other women paused to stare at her.

"Many men die in bed with their mistresses," Aine explained her presence. "I did not want O'Neill to die without me."

"We need to talk about that," Sunshine said. "But it will have to wait. So Elena wanted this money and her fifteen minutes of fame, so she conjured up a harpy? It takes more than that. She must have magic or otherworldly connections. Just any woman who wanted to win a contest couldn't summon a creature that's been nearly extinct for a thousand years or so."

O'Neill came back in the office. "If she's a witch, she didn't tell me. I confess that I don't know a lot about her.

We've only been together a short time. She's ambitious and passionate about her work. I'm sure anyone who could do it would kill their competition—or in this case, the people who decide who gets the money. I'm going to call Malto and have her pick up Elena."

"For what?" Sunshine asked him. "You can't prove she told the harpy what to do, and even if you could, no jury would convict her."

"But why would she want the shifters dead?" Jane asked quietly. "Are they artists too?"

"I don't know about Tom," Sunshine replied. "But Lloyd and Amos were in a band together. I suppose you could consider the tattoo guys artists, but not in Elena's league. John was certainly not involved in the arts. It doesn't make sense."

O'Neill took out his phone. "All the more reason to have Malto pick her up."

"That could be dangerous," Sunshine warned. "Even though Elena seems to be human, that doesn't mean she can't call the harpy if she needs to."

"We need to question her," he said. "She might have the answers."

"I agree. But we should go together and not chance one person dealing with a harpy by themselves. Unless you want to send Aine. I'm not worried about her since she's already dead."

They all stared at the *beane sidhe.*

"I would be pleased to bring Elena here so she could call the harpy. That would make this waiting more bearable."

Sunshine considered it, tapping her purple fingernail on the desktop. "No. We better not do that. What if there's something else involved that we aren't seeing? Even if Aine was okay, the harpy could turn on her summoner and kill Elena."

"Okay. Then we go together," O'Neill decided. "I'll leave Malto out of this one."

They agreed to travel to Elena's apartment without using his car.

"It will keep us from giving anything away," Sunshine said. "I'll take you with me. Aine has her own means of transportation."

"You mean flying?" O'Neill gulped. "Like on a broomstick or something?"

"Just grab your guns, honey." Sunshine grinned as she took his arm. "You'll be travelling first class with Air Sunshine. Trust me. It will be smooth as silk. You won't even know you're flying."

Jane giggled nervously. "What do you want me to do?"

"Just keep those shifters fed."

"You mean like pizza and stuff, right?" Jane paled.

"Definitely. Mouse isn't on their menu." Sunshine blew her a kiss. "This won't take long."

There was a knock at the front door. Tension immediately hit everyone in the office.

"You didn't order more pizza, did you?" Sunshine asked.

Jane shook her head, unable to speak without squeaking.

"I'll get it," O'Neill said.

He went to the door with Aine and Sunshine right behind him.

"Not that I think the harpy will politely knock before she comes in to kill us all," Sunshine whispered.

O'Neill unlocked the door. His hands tightly clutched the rifle.

Outside, Malto was being held in the air by the harpy's claws as the creature hovered above the street.

"She only wants to be left alone," Malto yelled. "She says she'll let me go if you stop chasing her."

O'Neill grimly raised one of the rifles, aiming for the harpy's human-looking head.

Malto screamed as the harpy's claws dug into her shoulders. She was dangling ten feet above the street, blood dripping down her sides.

"Please! I'm okay," Malto called out to him. "Put that away, or she'll kill me. Don't be stupid, Sean."

He slowly lowered the rifle. "What do you want?" he yelled at the harpy.

Her voice grated at their senses but her reply was understood. "Let me be. Soon I shall depart this place. Do not seek to find me again."

"No!" Sunshine muttered an incantation that made a large blue circle around the harpy and Malto. "Release her, and we will spare your life. Kill her, and you won't see another day."

The harpy cried out again but this time the high-pitched sound that came from her mouth was impossible for them to understand. She broke free from Sunshine's impromptu spell and started to fly away with her captive.

Malto screamed, and O'Neill fired the rifle, hitting the harpy in the back as she moved away from them. Sunshine tried another spell, but nothing seemed to stop her. Aine rode the air currents from the door to the spot where the harpy had been, but the creature had moved quickly, disappearing from sight.

"We have to do something," O'Neill yelled. "We can't just let her take Sharon."

Sunshine stood in the doorway with her eyes closed. "She's too powerful. We don't even really understand the magic she possesses. It died out so long ago that we don't know how to fight it."

"We need the woman—O'Neill's lover," Aine replied. "Once we have the summoner, she will be able to tell us where to find the creature. Quickly. Pull yourselves together. I am going to see Elena Spiros."

Sunshine wrapped her arms around O'Neill and followed Aine as they headed toward Elena's apartment. The sky was beginning to cloud up with a late afternoon thunderstorm from the heat and humidity of the day. Flashes of lightning accompanied them across town with the wind howling through the clouds around them.

It only took a moment to reach their destination. Aine was the first. When Sunshine and O'Neill arrived, Elena was cowering on her knees before the *beane sidhe.*

"Help me, Sean," Elena called out to him when she saw him arrive. She tried to reach him but Aine wouldn't let her move. "She's going to kill me."

O'Neill was shaken by his air travel with Sunshine. He tried to speak but couldn't get the words out. His stomach threatened to heave up his lunch. He held his head down and swallowed hard, focusing on the floor.

"What he's trying to say," Sunshine translated, "is that we know you called the harpy. You've had at least ten people killed so far to make your paintings famous. We know how you got the grant money. We want the creature."

"I won't tell you where she is," Elena said. "I-I'm not even sure I know anymore."

Aine lifted the woman straight up from the floor with one hand around her neck. "Tell us, and we may not kill you."

"Put her down," O'Neill commanded. "She's no good to us dead."

With a bleak scowl on her crone face, Aine dropped Elena to the hardwood floor.

He went to his lover's side. "You have to tell us where to find the harpy. She'll kill again if we don't stop her."

Elena's laugh was raspy from the pressure that had been applied to her throat. "You can't stop her. No one can. She's immortal, created by the ancient gods to serve as executioner for those who have done wrong."

"The people you killed to get that money and gallery exhibits didn't do anything wrong," Sunshine argued. "You had her kill for profit. That might not sit well with her once we explain."

"Go ahead. Knock yourselves out. Try to talk to

that…thing." Elena tossed her long, black hair. "The words I used to bring her here and bind her to my will don't work anymore. She's doing what she wants to do now. I'm done with her anyway."

"What did you say?" Sunshine demanded. "What were the words? How did you know how to call her?"

Elena's smile was cat-like on her beautiful face. "My ancestors were among those who created the first harpy. My lineage is that of the Olympian gods. You can't duplicate what I did. Ordinary magic doesn't cut it."

"Let's say that's true," O'Neill contended. "How do you undo it? How do you get rid of her? She's got my partner. Sharon Malto has never done anything to you. Tell me how to get her back."

"There's no point in getting her back, Sean. She's dead if the harpy has her. You can't save her." She smoothed her hand over his. "Just forget all this. I'm going to be a famous, wealthy artist. Stay with me."

Aine started toward her with murder in her eyes.

O'Neill held out a hand to stop her. "I understand that you have what you wanted. But that doesn't include me. I'll find some way to prosecute you for these murders. I'll see you behind bars."

"Don't be so dramatic—or so ethical. You can't pin those deaths on me. I can prove I was home during the ones out of the city, and nowhere near the ones that happened here."

"What about the other seven deaths?" Sunshine growled. "Where were you when my boyfriend was killed by your creature?"

Elena stared angrily at the three of them. "I only had the creature kill three people who were standing between me and what I deserved. The other deaths were all on her. I don't know why she kept killing, and I don't know how to stop her. She's out of my control. Now if you'll excuse me, I'm late for a luncheon."

Sunshine turned her head away, her hair showing her anger and frustration by frizzing around her face. O'Neill put down his rifle and started toward the door.

"And this is justice in your world?" Aine asked. "We leave her unharmed though she is a murderess? This will not stand."

Elena screamed as Aine flew at her. The *beane sidhe* lifted her by the throat again, shook her like a rag doll, and then tossed her against the wall.

"Never cross my path again, murderess," Aine warned. "Never seek Sean O'Neill again. If you do, I vow swift and painful retribution."

Aine flew out the window, her gray robe billowing in the wind. Sunshine took hold of O'Neill and followed. The three were back in the outer office of the detective agency in moments.

"Maybe she was lying," Jane argued when they'd explained what had happened. "Maybe you should go back and question her again."

O'Neill shook his head, his teeth chattering as he tried to recover from the wild ride through the sky.

"She's not lying," Sunshine said. "Between me and Aine, we'd know. She lost control of the harpy. She's just an amateur with a god complex. She doesn't know what to do either."

"We must find a way to track and kill the harpy," Aine said. "It is not impossible. The hard part is finding her."

"I still think she'll come here for these two." Sunshine gestured to the sleeping shifters. "For whatever reason, she wants them dead. She's hoping we'll come for Malto, but she's overestimating our abilities. We still have to wait for her to come to us."

"But why would she continue killing past her summoning?" Aine questioned. "And why this worthless lot? We are missing a large piece of this puzzle."

"I don't know." Sunshine sank into one of the purple

chairs in the outer office. "I can't figure it out, but we don't know much about harpies either. Maybe they just lose it sometimes."

Aine shook her head. "I have never known it to happen, albeit your words are true. I only saw a harpy once when I was very young. I thought it to be the last of her kind."

"So what do we do?" O'Neill was finally capable of speech.

"It seems we wait." Aine sat too.

"No." Jane wrung her hands. "We can't wait. We have to do something. There's an answer somewhere. We have to find it before Malto dies."

"No doubt she is dead already," Aine said.

"I don't know." Sunshine's fine brows knit together above her sharp eyes. "Maybe there is something. Aine—you have the ability to command Tom and Lloyd to tell you the truth. Maybe we can squeeze something from them."

"When you say squeeze," O'Neill queried, "you don't mean kill, right?"

"No. Of course not," she assured him. "But if the old legends are true, a *beane sidhe* can only be of *Fae* blood. She can make them remember everything they've ever seen or done. I could do it too, but it would take a strong spell, and we may not have time for that."

"Can you do it?" he asked Aine. "Without killing them?"

She nodded. "It can be done with little or no damage to them."

Aine went to Tom but didn't awaken him. Instead she put her hand against his head and closed her eyes. "Show me everything you have seen and done in recent days."

"Can you see anything?" Jane whispered.

"Quiet!" Aine said.

Jane moved away from her but didn't leave the outer office.

Aine searched through the young man's memories, not exactly sure what she was looking for, and yet feeling there was something there. There was a great hodgepodge of events and people in Tom's mind. It was difficult to find something so small as to be almost unnoticeable.

She saw Amos Johnson and Lloyd Samson standing on a dark street corner with Tom and a few others she guessed at being shapeshifters. She recognized the man from *Tattoo Hell* who'd been killed.

"Wait!" she finally called out. "I think I may know what has caused the harpy to hunt down and kill these shifters. Why did we not think of it before?"

"Just keep those shifters fed."

Chapter Twenty-three

"What is it?" O'Neill demanded.

"I must see what the other lad saw as well." Aine left Tom and went to Lloyd.

"Can't you at least give us a hint?" Sunshine said.

"A hint?" Aine frowned as she puzzled over the words.

"Never mind." O'Neill shook his head. "Just look at Lloyd's thoughts."

"Hurry!" Jane excitedly hopped from one foot to another.

Aine knew where to look in Lloyd's sleeping thoughts and found the same night. She opened her eyes at once and withdrew from his mind. "The shifters—including your wolf—were privileged to see something very few have ever seen. Alas, it also caused their deaths."

Sunshine gripped the arm of her chair until her knuckles were white. "What's that?"

"The harpy has a nest with an egg in it. She sensed the

intruders and has gone after them. No one shall live to tell the tale of her motherhood."

"She has a nest?" Jane squeaked. "And an egg? So there will be two of them?" Undone by the idea, she reverted to her true form and ran into the kitchen to hide.

"Where is she?" Sunshine got slowly to her feet. "I don't care if she's in line to be mother of the year. I'm going to kill her."

But Aine wasn't familiar with the area she'd seen in the city. She couldn't relate what she'd seen as a place to hunt the harpy. "Perhaps if I could show one of you what I've seen."

"Sounds like a good idea. Asleep, right?"

"That would be preferable."

"No reason to use fresh meat." Sunshine snapped her fingers and half caught O'Neill as he fell to the floor asleep.

"I gave him my word that you would not use magic on him again." Aine helped her carry him to the sofa. "You gave your word as well."

"Technically, I'm not guilty of using *new* magic on him. I already used the sleep spell before we promised not to do it again." Sunshine shrugged. "It was already there. All I had to do was activate it."

Aine frowned at her. "I do not like your cunning, not when it comes to O'Neill."

"It's already done. And he'll thank us for it if we can find Malto still alive. Get in there and do what you need to do."

Half agreeing with her and knowing speed was of the essence, Aine went into O'Neill's sleeping mind. It was faster than it had been with the shifters since she had been here before.

He was waiting for her. "She did it again, didn't she?"

"She had good reason."

"Okay. Show me where the nest is. I'll settle up afterward with her."

Aine reached inside her thoughts and showed him the place she'd seen the shifters find the harpy's nest. "Do you know it?"

"Sure. It's only a few blocks from here, on the other side of the Wells Fargo building. She probably had to stay close to Elena. Let's go."

After Aine emerged from O'Neill's unconscious mind, Sunshine rapidly awakened him with a few sharp slaps to the face. "We don't have time for you to snooze all day."

"I think I should drop you in the harpy's nest after I get Malto out of it."

"Ignore your petty disagreements," Aine warned. "No doubt she is waiting for us. If we are to take her, it must be swiftly, or you risk death."

O'Neill flatly refused to fly anywhere again with Sunshine. He took the rifles and left in his car. Aine and Sunshine went with him. They had to face the harpy together if they had a chance of rescuing Malto.

"Not only is this slower than we had to be," Sunshine complained. "It's the ugliest car I've ever seen."

"At least mine isn't in the impound lot with shifter blood all over it." He shook his head as he put on the lights and siren to run through a red light. "I can't believe I even said that."

Sunshine was in front with him. Aine had chosen to ride in back. She tried to stay focused on the task ahead of them.

She'd seen a harpy hunted once, and the lives it had taken before the thing was dead. There had been an army at that time so long ago. She feared there was not enough of her group to lose so many in this battle.

At that time she had been a young queen. She was of little use to the hunters who'd killed the harpy. Now she might be the only one who could withstand the creature's attack.

They reached the area where Aine had seen the nest. It was in a sheltered spot between two large stone buildings, a steel overhang protecting it from the wind and rain.

"I recognized this area because of the graffiti," O'Neill said as he parked the car and took out the rifles. "It's pretty good if you like street art. I can see why the harpy might be drawn here."

They stared at the vision of trees and mountains rendered in multi-colored chalk that had been meticulously drawn on the walls and alley below the nest area. There were drawings of various Greek gods and goddesses with their arms raised to Mount Olympus.

"Who has done this thing?" Aine asked. "It is truly a work of beauty."

Sunshine laughed. "Don't tell the people who have to clean it."

"Look up there." O'Neill pointed to the nest. "How did the shifters even find it?"

"They probably didn't," Sunshine conjectured. "See that spot on the upper roof? Sometimes the shifters hang out there. That's probably what happened. John and Marcus and their friends didn't even realize what they were close to. She killed them for nothing. They wouldn't have bothered her nest."

"The same could be said for the mother bear's den or the tiger's home," Aine replied. "They do not take risks when it comes to their young."

Sunshine and Aine went up a rusted fire escape that brought them close to the nest. O'Neill waited on the ground with the rifle poised to fire if the harpy returned. The nest was large—at least five feet by five feet. It was made of a thousand scraps of wood, metal, and cloth that the harpy had found throughout the city. Some of the cloth was still identifiable as a banner from a local restaurant.

"Is Malto up there?" O'Neill asked.

"She's here," Sunshine answered, carefully lowering herself into the large nest. "She's still alive but badly injured. She can't survive the harpy's poison."

"And there is an egg." Aine held up an egg the size of a football. It was heavily armored, a dull shade of cobalt blue and gray in the sunlight. "Shall I toss it to the street?"

"No!" O'Neill and Sunshine yelled at the same time.

"We don't know if it's ready to come out and start slashing," O'Neill reasoned.

"The two of you take it back to the office," Sunshine said. "If I don't get Malto to a witch healer quickly, she'll die."

"Witch healer?" O'Neill questioned. "The hospital is five minutes away."

"They won't do her any good," Sunshine gently explained. "You have to trust me on this if you want to keep your partner."

"All right. I guess I don't have any choice." O'Neill scanned the area around them. "Whatever we're gonna do, let's do it, and get out of here."

Aine helped Sunshine gather Malto's unconscious body close to her. "Where do you go, Sunshine? To the red witch queen?"

"No. My family can heal her—I hope." Her eyes met Aine's, filled with grim determination. "Don't let this party get started until I get back."

Not sure what she was talking about—there could hardly be a party with the creature still on the loose—Aine nodded. She took the harpy's egg and started back down the fire escape. Sunshine closed her eyes, held tightly to Malto, and vanished.

O'Neill grabbed the egg from Aine and studied it. "All those people dead for this?"

"What harm would you visit on those you feared might kill your offspring?" She took the egg back from him. "Hurry. The harpy won't be gone long. The egg is soon to hatch."

They got back in the car and headed toward the agency. With Sunshine gone, they were a person short of the effort they needed to fight the harpy. Aine had her own magic, but it wasn't as practical as Sunshine's. She could move them, and the egg, to where the harpy couldn't find them, but she had precious few other resources.

O'Neill put on his lights and siren, driving like a madman through the streets of downtown Norfolk. But they were only on the road for a few minutes when they heard the harpy's screeching cry that was followed by her talons scraping the metal roof.

"I don't think her claws can get through that." He flashed a frightened frown at his companion. "Good thing we don't have the convertible, huh?"

The harpy continued her assault against the car. At first her talons only scratched the roof, but after a few passes, they actually began slicing through the thin metal. The process must have seemed too slow, however, for the harpy. She began smashing her body against the windows.

Aine looked into the creature's eyes as she damaged the window next to her face. The harpy was enraged, furious with the need to reclaim her egg. The glass next to her didn't shatter, but one more pass might have seen the creature in the car with them.

"A sword! It has been many years since I longed for my sword."

O'Neill put his service revolver in her hand. "Just point and fire. It's not hard. Even if you don't kill her, it should scare her off."

She glanced at the odd weapon then saw the angry harpy coming toward her window again. Without another thought, she fired at the creature, shattering the window, glass flying everywhere.

"You should've opened the window," he said. "Now you've done what she couldn't. Shoot her again."

Aine kept firing the weapon until the harpy was gone. "She'll be back. She won't abandon her egg. She'll follow us to the building with the purple door where the shifters are.

But now we don't have magic."

"Let's not worry about that right now," he advised. "If we can make it in the building, we can take out the assault rifles. I don't know if those will kill her, but they should make her think twice about coming after us."

"I hope Sunshine returns swiftly." Her eyes remained on the sky.

There was still no sign of the harpy all the way back to the Purple Door Detective Agency. Despite Aine's misgivings of their positions in this battle, she took the egg inside while O'Neill gathered his weapons and followed her.

He locked the front door behind him. "I don't think this lock is going to matter to her." He looked at the terrified shifters. "Get some furniture here and put it up against the door. Jane, find something to cover the windows."

"Where's Sunshine?" she asked with a tremor in her voice.

"She is unharmed," Aine told her. "Do not fear or become a mouse. She has gone to have O'Neill's partner healed. We need your human hands to fight the harpy."

Jane pointed at the egg. "Is that what I think it is?"

"A harpy egg," Aine confirmed. "The creature will no doubt move heaven and earth to have it back. We must do our best to stop her."

"What can I do?"

"Do as O'Neill commands. Find furniture to put in front of the windows. I am going to hide the egg." She stormed into Mr. Bad's office. "You are the only one who can do what is necessary with this egg."

"I'm sure you can hide it without me."

"You understand and yet fail to react. You must take this egg to the underworld where it can be hidden for all time. This task can only be yours."

"Don't think I will give away my hiding place here to keep humans from dying. Leave the egg here with me if you must, but reclaim it after you have dealt with the harpy. With

Miss Merryweather gone, the chances of survival are limited."

"I know that, my lord. Your aid in this fight would be greatly appreciated."

There was no response. Aine left the egg on the desk and quietly closed the door behind her.

Chapter Twenty-four

The harpy began her assault on the building with a fierce battle cry. She ignored the roof and began throwing herself at the windows on the ground floor.

Jane immediately turned into a mouse and went to hide in the supply closet, but she'd made it through the process of blocking the windows, which was what Aine had asked of her.

Both shifters stood in the middle of the front office area ready for the fight. Tom had shifted completely into the large lion with a tawny mane and frightened eyes. Lloyd had become a sleek black panther. He flexed his muscles, showed his teeth, and growled.

O'Neill was nervously tapping his finger on one of the assault rifles as he watched them change. When Aine came out of Mr. Bad's office, he nodded to the shifters. "Maybe one of them could've stayed a person and I could've showed him how to fire a rifle. I don't know what good they're going to be this way."

Aine nodded. "I will speak to them. But have no fear, neither will attack you."

"Yeah." He watched the big cats again. "Thanks for that."

Tom volunteered to become human again when Aine spoke to him. She had O'Neill explain how to use the large rifle that had been on one of the purple chairs.

"Don't bother asking me." Lloyd's voice was more like a roar. "If I have to fight, I'm fighting this way."

The harpy screamed and threw herself against the front door. It vibrated on its hinges but stayed in place. The creature made a circle around the building, trying the windows and clawing at the bricks.

Aine held the reloaded revolver that O'Neill had given her in the car. She longed for a sword or a spear. The police weapon had only frightened the harpy. As far as she could tell, it had done no lasting damage.

The harpy she'd seen die had been beheaded, after hundreds of other wounds. It had been done with a charmed blade. Perhaps if Sunshine got back in time, she could conjure one up. Aine had the strength to use it against the creature but no magic that would defeat her.

She thought about Mr. Bad brooding in his dark office. She also considered that the harpy's death was unfortunate. Though the creature had killed, it was through no fault of her own when she was under the control of O'Neill's lover. Protecting her offspring—perhaps the last of her kind— seemed not so much a crime to her.

A dozen bricks fell from the outside wall of the agency as the harpy determinedly continued her onslaught. The windows rattled in their casements, and the door threatened to give way.

"I don't think she can get in the elevator." Jane managed to become a person again. "It's magical and made of metal. I think we should go in the elevator."

Lloyd roared his approval of the idea. O'Neill kept his eyes and his rifle focused on the front door.

Tom wiped nervous perspiration from his eyes. "I think the mouse is right. We can't win against this thing. If she gets in, we're done for."

O'Neill glanced at Aine. "What do you think?"

"Without knowing the magic that works the elevator, I would rather stay and fight. The metal box could become your tomb."

"That's right. You can't die, so you have no dog in this fight. Maybe this is my death that you foresaw."

Tom, Jane, and Lloyd all stared at the *beane sidhe*.

"As long as you are living, I fight for your life." Aine's green eyes were steady on his.

"Okay. Thanks."

The harpy smashed into one of the front windows. The impact shattered the glass and left a gaping hole in the wall. The three men—Lloyd became human again to use his hands—quickly pushed a large metal file cabinet in front of it.

"You got another gun like that?" Tom asked O'Neill.

"Yes but no ammo. Sorry. I wish I did. Are there any other things we could use as weapons?" O'Neill turned to Jane.

"If the harpy comes inside, she will kill all of you," Aine said. "Right now she is only taunting us. She could have come through the wall at any time."

"Yeah. Thanks for that." Tom began his transformation back into the lion.

Lloyd said, "Now I know how they felt at the Alamo."

"Not a great way to keep up morale," O'Neill told Aine.

"I spoke the truth," she defended.

Jane trembled. "Sometimes it's better to keep the truth to yourself."

A bright light in the outer office heralded Sunshine's return. She smiled at everyone gathered there. "I'm so glad you made it back," she said to Aine and O'Neill. "I didn't even stay long enough to get my face healed."

"What about Malto?" he asked.

"She's going to be fine," she told him. "She won't remember a thing. She thinks she had the flu and had to take some time off. I tucked her in at her apartment. I even conjured a few roses from you wishing her a speedy recovery."

He laughed. "Thanks, but Malto hates roses. She's gonna think I lost my mind."

"Oh well. Better that than being dead from harpy poison." She glanced around the room as the harpy threw herself against the wall again. "How's it going here?"

"I hid the egg," Aine said. "You should have allowed them to heal your face. It is very angry."

Sunshine put her hand up but didn't touch the raw mark on her cheek. "I thought you might need me here. I'm not going to die from this scratch just yet. I hope it can wait until after we get rid of this thing."

"What do we do now?" O'Neill asked. "Do you have magic covered bullets? How does it work?"

Jane quivered. "Shouldn't we all get in the elevator?"

As she said it, the electricity went off. It was barely dusk outside but the inner office got dark.

"I really think we should get in the elevator," she said again.

"That won't help," Sunshine told her. "It takes magic to make it run. I need all the magic I have to release on the harpy."

"I think we should go outside and shoot her," Lloyd said. "What's the point of hiding in here? She's just going to come in and kill us."

"No," Aine said. "No one leaves the castle when it is under siege."

There was a loud rumbling from beneath them. The sound grew louder as it came closer.

"Upstairs!" Sunshine yelled.

But it was too late.

The harpy came under the building, through the floor, with a screech that shook the structure. Her eyes glanced around the room until they fell on Sunshine. She grabbed the witch by the shoulders and started digging back out through the floor.

O'Neill and Lloyd began firing. It was difficult to tell if they were hitting anything. Ruptured wood and stone had spewed up with the harpy. The waiting room was covered with it.

Aine didn't think twice. She threw herself down the hole after them. The bullets meant nothing to her. She grabbed the harpy's scaled leg and pulled hard. Her strength was enough that she jerked the creature backward. The harpy raked her arms with her other foot but found there was nothing there to injure.

Once the harpy was back in the office, Aine beat at her midsection with her fists, trying to make her release Sunshine. With no magic—only her inability not to die—all she could do was keep the creature immobilized.

"Shoot it!" she called out. "O'Neill, shoot the creature now."

"You're in the way," he yelled back. "She's moving too fast. I'll shoot you too."

The harpy freed one clawed hand from its grasp on the witch and raked it across Aine's face. Jane gasped as she saw the damage done, but before the creature could move again, Aine had transformed into the crone.

"You cannot defeat me by changing shape," the harpy hissed at her. "I shall have the witch's life. There's nothing you can do to prevent it."

Aine already knew that the deep gouges into the Sunshine's chest and back could be the death of her, yet she held on to the harpy with fierce strength. "You underestimate me. Your cries are those of a mewling child compared to mine."

The death cry of the *beane sidhe* fell on the ears of those around her like a bomb going off. O'Neill finally began shooting at the creature as Aine kept the harpy at bay while it writhed, trying to escape the sound that came from her opponent.

All three shifters fell to the floor with their hands over their ears. Both cats cried out in pain as they were exposed to the unearthly sound.

Still the harpy clutched Sunshine, her claws sinking deeper into the witch's flesh. She kept tearing at Aine, even though it was evident there was no human body to assail.

Aine knew this was all she could do. She didn't have Sunshine's practical magic that could form a sword or an elevator to defeat the creature. O'Neill and Lloyd kept firing their rifles, joined a moment later by Tom. The bullets bounced off the iron hide of the harpy, inflicting little, if any, damage. Their strength together could only keep the creature from taking Sunshine and departing through the floor again.

"That's enough!"

No one was certain at first who had shouted the words. The tone and voice penetrated both the harpy's screams and the *beane sidhe's* wail. It even pierced the staccato of gunfire in the room.

Aine looked back and saw Mr. Bad emerging from his office. He was as she remembered from long ago when she'd been stripped of her right to rest in the quiet of the underworld. Centuries later, he hadn't changed.

He stalked across the room, easily eight feet tall with black skin and blacker hair. His eyes were made of the night that he'd witnessed for ten thousand years trapped in the underworld created by his brother, Zeus, who sought to keep him from the earth.

One large hand reached down and easily held the harpy. "You will not take her. It is not her time. And you can no longer remain here."

Aine pulled Sunshine close to her and signaled for O'Neill to stop shooting. She didn't need to bother—he, Lloyd, and Tom were transfixed by the ancient god in their midst. They had stopped firing as soon as they'd seen him. The mouse and the lion lay down before the might of the one they'd jokingly called Mr. Bad.

"I only want what's mine," the harpy lisped. "They took it from me. I won't leave until I have it."

Midnight eyes focused on the creature nearly as ancient as himself. His hand slowly stroked the metallic wings and scaled body. "You have been wronged, as have all your ancestors. You will leave this place and not return, but you will not leave alone."

He glanced toward his office, and the egg came to him. He placed it in the harpy's claws.

"Thank you, dark lord." The harpy bowed her head. "Happily shall I leave this realm now and never be summoned again."

"So it shall be." Hades looked around at the faces that dared gaze upon him. O'Neill knew no better. Aine had nothing to fear. The shifters had hidden their eyes from him.

"What are you waiting for, Aine?" he asked. "You know I have no power to heal. Take Miss Merryweather to her family. Tend her well. She must survive."

"My lord." Aine respectfully inclined her head to him. She took a quick glance at O'Neill, still holding his rifle, and then rose to ride the wind to the place the witch had last visited.

"Uh...excuse me," O'Neill interrupted. "Are you a witch too?"

The trembling words amused the elder god. He smiled, despite the arrogance it took to speak to him—or perhaps it was courage. "No. I am not a witch. I leave that to Miss Merryweather. Good day to you, young sir."

O'Neill watched him disappear through the floor with the harpy and the egg before he lost consciousness.

Aine looked back and saw Mr. Bad emerging from his office.

Chapter Twenty-five

Three weeks later, Sunshine Merryweather returned to her purple-doored home. Jane hugged her and cried when she saw her.

"Everyone's gone—I was glad to see the cats go! But I wasn't sure if I had enough food to last. I even thought about going to the grocery store myself, but I was waiting until the last seed was gone. I'm so glad you're back."

Sunshine frowned at the huge mess still waiting for her. She closed her eyes and shrugged. As she did, so did the old building. When it was over, things were back in place, including the floor, outside bricks, and the front window. "There we are. Where is everyone?"

"If you mean Aine, I haven't seen her since she took you to Wilmington. By the way, you look wonderful. I'm so glad your family was able to heal you."

"My Aunt Molly said I was in pretty bad shape when Aine brought me there. I'm glad they'd met before. I don't know what would've happened if she'd shown up with me like that before she had a chance to explain."

"Well, she never came back. I waited. O'Neill called a few times and came over here a few other times. He hasn't heard anything from her either."

The door was open to Mr. Bad's office. Sunshine went closer to it and peered into the darkness.

"He's gone too," Jane explained. "After he showed his real form, he took the harpy and the egg with him and disappeared. It was like some mass exodus from the agency. I didn't know what to say or do. That's why I'm so glad to see you. And there's the food situation. But I guess I mentioned that."

"You did." Sunshine sat in her purple office chair and kicked off her purple pumps. "Any business calls?"

"Yes. Dozens of them. Do you want me to get them before you go shopping?"

Considering the question, Sunshine absently rubbed the place where the harpy had slashed her. There was nothing to mar her smooth complexion, but she could still feel it. Her aunt had told her it was all in her mind. Sunshine knew she'd forget it after a while, but it was part of an experience that had changed her life. It would take some time.

Not only had John been killed but Mr. Bad had finally revealed himself after five years. She had no idea who he was until the day he'd saved her life—although she should've guessed from Aine's questions about him.

Meeting Aine had been part of that experience. She'd hoped the *beane sidhe* would stay on as her associate. Her strength and determination had also played a part in making sure Sunshine had survived the harpy. The last thing she remembered was seeing Aine's face before she'd held her tight and taken her to Wilmington. She really didn't want to lose that friendship. Why would she have disappeared, even out of O'Neill's life, after she'd come so far to find him?

The answer was obvious, of course, to everyone but

Aine herself. Sunshine briefly wondered where she'd gone, but that too seemed to have an easy answer.

She glanced at Mr. Bad's office again and questioned if he'd return. She had a million things to say to him. But he wouldn't be as easy as Aine to find.

"Sunshine?" Jane asked, moving so she was in her face. "Are you going shopping? It's been days since I had any cereal."

"Sure. I'm going shopping, and then I'm going to get O'Neill. Can you keep things going for just a little longer? I promise I'll be back as soon as I can."

Jane nibbled at her fingernail. "Okay. Will you drop the food off first?"

* * *

Police detectives Sean O'Neill and Sharon Malto were bringing in a man who'd been wanted for the last ten years. He was accused of killing his best friend, a man he'd grown up with. They'd received a good tip on a cold case that was going to make their captain smile.

As they were dragging the man up the stairs and into the Norfolk Police Office, Sunshine Merryweather appeared next to O'Neill and tapped him on the shoulder.

He almost lost his grip on the struggling killer. "Hey. Can't you just walk up like everyone else? I'm busy. Maybe later."

"Is she back again?" Malto demanded in an irritated tone. "I think she gave me the flu. You know, you're gonna get a reputation if you go out with a new girlfriend every other week."

"We need to take a road trip," Sunshine said, her eyes focused on O'Neill. "There's someone who needs to see you."

"Aine? Did you find her?"

"Another one?" Malto said. "Forget it. You've already gone past having a reputation."

"I know where she is. She won't come back unless we

go get her."

The happy expression on O'Neill's face disappeared. "I'm not dragging her back here if she doesn't want to be my *beane sidhe* anymore. I was getting through life just fine without her singing my death song every five minutes and changing back and forth on what she looks like. Besides, I've got work to do."

"This will only take a few minutes," Sunshine assured him. "I'm sure Detective Malto would be glad to do the paperwork on this perp for you."

"What are you talking about?" Malto questioned. "I'm not doing the paperwork so Romeo here can go find some other lovesick female to hang out with."

"I won't make you go, O'Neill," Sunshine said. "If you say no and mean it, I'm out of here. But you'll regret it the rest of whatever life you have."

He stared into her flashing eyes. "I know. I've known since that first night in my apartment."

"Okay. That's enough for me. I don't want to know any more." Malto grabbed the killer by the scruff of his neck. "Come on, you. I'd rather do the paperwork than have to hear about O'Neill's weird love life."

Sunshine smiled and thanked Detective Malto. "How are you feeling? I hope you got over the flu without any other complications."

"Yeah. I feel okay. I've had a few strange dreams about flying, and I keep smelling sage. But otherwise, I'm good. Get out of here, O'Neill. I'll see you tomorrow."

He went with Sunshine toward the side of the building until they found a quiet spot near a dumpster. She put her hand on his shoulder.

"Before we go, my car hasn't been released from impound," she told him. "How much longer is that going to take?"

"Considering that I can't tell anyone what really happened and Irene Godfrey's death remains unsolved, I'd say three to six months."

"Anything you can do to speed it up?"

"This isn't a parking ticket, Sunshine. It takes what it takes."

"Just checking. Okay. Let's go."

A few minutes later, O'Neill found himself in unfamiliar surroundings. Parts of a once great castle, now abandoned and falling to rubble, towered near him. The ruins were set on a hill overlooking a large body of water. The stones were covered in emerald green moss and tiny, purple flowers. Trees and shrubs grew up between the stones and lichen that covered almost everything else.

He checked his cell phone—no signal. Sunshine was gone. He wasn't exactly sure what he was doing there except for a single imperative—bring his *beane sidhe* back where she belonged. "All I have to do is figure out how to find her." But he didn't have to worry about searching for her. It only took a moment for Aine to feel his presence.

"Castle O'Neill, I guess." He shrugged and glanced around himself. "Is that the ocean over there?"

"Shane's Castle," she corrected. "Built in 1345 by a member of the O'Neill family. The name was changed in 1722 by Shane McBrien O'Neill. The loch is Loch Neagh. Your ancestor, Hugh O'Neill, left here in 1730 aboard a ship bound for America. But this was his home."

"Amazing! His eyes stayed on her.

"But you did not come for a history lesson. What are you doing here?" She also glanced around. "Did Sunshine bring you to this place?"

"Yes. And I'm not sure how I'm going to get back—I didn't bring my passport. I guess I'll appeal to the U.S. Embassy and tell them I was mugged or something. Better that than flying anywhere with her again. That witch is crazy."

He smiled as he spoke to her, his gaze resting lightly on her face, happy to see her.

"I understand how you came, but I do not understand why you are here, O'Neill."

"You can't stay here." He swallowed hard and then launched into the rest of it. "I need you with me, right? How else am I going to learn the secrets of the *beane sidhe* and have someone warn me when I'm about to die? How will I get to the underworld?"

She looked away from him toward the distant shore. "With your work, I would be singing to warn you of death every day. I fear I am not up to the task. Go home. Be fortunate in your life. I shall be at your side when you die."

Aine turned away from him. There was as much for her here in the rotting pile of stone as there was in Norfolk. This wasn't her home either, but she had no wish to be disgraced in her final task for the family she served.

O'Neill took her hand, and she immediately became the young queen—innocent and vulnerable—before she had been a wife and a mother, before she was a warrior that had led her people.

"I want to get to know you." She started to speak, but he kept going. "I know this isn't the real you anymore, *yada, yada, yada.* I don't care. Yes, I like seeing you like this, but I want to know those other parts of you too."

"To what end?" Tears misted her eyes. "I have been dead longer than this castle. I am the harbinger of death. Why would you want to spend time with me?"

He moved closer to her, careful not to release her hand, and touched her beautiful face, catching a lock of her fiery red hair with his fingers. "Because I've never met anyone like you, and I want to know everything you can teach me. I want to be with you, Aine. Is that so difficult to believe?"

"No. You should be with your own. You should fall in love and marry, produce many offspring. My heart cannot bear another loss."

"I thought you wanted me to die and get it over with so you'd be free of your curse."

"Aye. That is what I want." She put her hand on his face and smiled back at him. "But I fear that would be more painful to me right now than lying in my tomb without knowing you."

"Great. So we have an understanding. No dire warnings of death while I'm working, and you don't step between me and the bullet unless you have some prior knowledge that it's going to kill me."

"I shall do my best." She laughed at him dictating terms to her, but she was glad to go back with him to that other foolish world. "And you, O'Neill, will do your best to live a long, prosperous life."

"You bet." He lightly kissed her lips. "Probably not as long as yours, but maybe Sunshine can give me a magic youth booster every now and again. And when we go, we both go."

"That may be so." Her smile showed a small dimple in her chin.

"Let's go." He scratched his head. "It's gonna take me a while to get out of Ireland."

She put her arms around him and carefully drew him close. "No, O'Neill. It will take little time at all. Hold on to me."

"With pleasure."

* * *

Six weeks later, Sunshine Merryweather was reading the newspaper and swearing at it—her usual habit in the morning when there were no clients in the outer office.

"Bad news?" Jane set a cup of tea on the desk in front of her.

"They're going to be working on the road out here in front of the office for the next six months. I'm going to have to buy a cover for my car so it doesn't stay dusty all the time. Not to mention that the one-way parking is bad enough on Brooke Street without them tearing it up."

"Could you not simply keep the dust from the vehicle

with magic?" Aine joined them in her black cloak.

"I could, but it's a waste of my energy to keep up with something like that." Sunshine put down the newspaper and took a sip of tea. "Here's a news flash I wanted both of you to see."

She pointed at the glass board that appeared. "It seems Elena Spiros has taken a turn for the worse in her career."

The beautiful artist was shown on the screen as she was arrested for art fraud at the D. C. celebration of her work.

A sallow-faced newsman narrated. "Miss Spiros was arrested when judges found that her original paintings had been done over stolen art that has been missing from the Metropolitan Museum of Art in New York." The news announcer filled in the details. "She could serve up to one hundred years for the theft. Spiros had risen quickly to fame by receiving one of the largest grants ever given by the National Endowment for the Arts."

"An interesting and cunning retribution," Aine acknowledged.

"We couldn't get her any other way," Sunshine said. "But at least she won't walk free after having those people killed."

Aine's cell phone rang. She briefly studied it and then threw it on the floor. "I shall not learn to carry this infernal device as O'Neill requests. No one needs to communicate with another so dearly."

Jane hurried to pick up the phone and tapped the screen to answer the call. "Purple Door Detective Agency."

"Why are you answering this, Jane?" O'Neill asked. "Put Aine on."

"She threw it on the floor again," Jane said. "Is there something you want me to tell her?"

"Yeah. Tell them both. Someone ran into a creature downtown. I don't want to speculate on what it is, but it looks part dragon and part man. He's not dead. Not even injured as far as I can tell. I think this should be right down your alley. I'm here now. Come on down and join the media circus."

"Tell him we are arriving shortly," Aine said.

"She said—"

"I heard. Tell her—"

Sunshine waved her hand at the phone, and it went dead. "You two need a secretary. You can't have Jane. Come on. Let's go. I hope that isn't Caeford. I'd hate to lose his monthly account."

"Don't forget that we need cereal," Jane called out from the kitchen.

"I won't forget," Sunshine said as she started to follow Aine out of the building.

A warm breeze floated past her. It smelled of summer and sea. She glanced sharply toward the office that had been empty since the day the harpy had almost killed her. The door had remained open, but now it was tightly closed.

She smiled as she walked by it, laying her hand against it.

"Are you changing clothes again?" Aine asked from the front door. "I do not understand why you feel the urge to use different clothing every day."

"Not changing clothes. And I'm right behind you. I just had to say hello to an old friend."

About the Authors

Joyce and Jim Lavene write award-winning, bestselling mystery and urban fantasy fiction as themselves, J.J. Cook, and Ellie Grant. Their first mystery novel, Last Dance, won the Master's Choice Award for best first mystery novel in 1999. Their romance, Flowers in the Night, was nominated for the Frankfurt Book Award in 2000.

They have written and published more than 70 novels for Harlequin, Penguin, Amazon, and Simon and Schuster that are sold worldwide. They have also published hundreds of non-fiction articles for national and regional publications. They live in Midland, North Carolina with their family and their rescue pets—Rudi, Stan Lee, and Quincy.

Visit them at:
www.joyceandjimlavene.com
www.facebook.com/joyceandjimlavene
http://amazon.com/author/jlavene
https://twitter.com/AuthorJLavene

Made in the USA
Middletown, DE
26 October 2015